# LOVE IS AT THE TABLE

## DARCI BALOGH

Knowhere Media LLC Denver CO

*To Dad.*

*For your love of ping pong and horseshoes, for sharing your knowledge of birds, for the music, the art, and the fun you always bring to the table.*

*And for bringing the unforgettable production of 'The Pirates and the Pilgrims' to life!*

*Thank you, Dad, for all of the Thanksgivings, holidays and regular days you've made so special throughout my life. And thank you for teaching me to be creative, to love knowledge and to laugh.*

"Love is a noun or a verb, it's something you do." Jenny scowled out the windshield as she drove and complained to her brother. "Love is not a name, okay? Nobody is called *Love*. That's stupid. Like being called Excitement or Hate."

"What about Joy? There are people named Joy," Jimmy responded. "I worked with a Joy once. She was nice."

Jenny rolled her eyes for the hundredth time since she'd picked him up at his condo. The four hour drive to their parent's vacation home in Iowa was nearing its end.

During the drive they had covered many topics of conversation; the fact that she'd chosen to wear her work slacks instead of something more comfy, his new haircut, pop music, his marital status—newly separated, and her love life—currently stagnant, but Jenny had focused most of her talking points on the woman their widower father had married a few months ago, Love Hathaway. A woman neither she nor Jimmy had met. A woman who would be playing hostess over Thanksgiving with their Dad at their family's beloved Lake House retreat.

Jenny had reluctantly agreed to spend one whole week with this Love person at the place her mother had made into their home away from home. Now that the week was about to begin she was having a hard time accepting the whole situation.

"It just...it just sticks in my craw," Jenny said.

Jimmy laughed out loud, "Why are you talking like a farm-house grandma?"

"I don't know," she answered. His amusement made her smile, revealing the small gap in her front teeth, the one she'd inherited from her Mom. "I get this way when I leave the city."

"Well, I don't care what her name is as long as she's a good fit for Dad," Jimmy said, always the level headed one. "And don't roll your eyes at that. Don't you want him to be happy?"

"Yes," Jenny admitted with an exasperated growl. "But how can he possibly know her well enough to be happy?"

Their Dad had married Love only 18 months after their mother passed away. Not even two years! In Jenny's opinion, that was not long enough to get over a 42 year marriage.

Jimmy gave her a one shouldered shrug and took a sip out of his travel mug. "I guess we'll find out this week."

"I don't understand how you're so blasé about it."

"He's a grown man, Jen, you can't stop him from getting remarried."

She glowered at his comment and they drove in silence for a few minutes. It was early afternoon and not a cloud in the sky. The landscape had changed drastically from downtown Chicago. Her sedan cruised through rolling hills dotted with quaint farmhouses and giant bales of hay, all surrounded by trees and shrubs in full fall foliage. The colors were brilliant.

"What if she's after his money?" she asked.

"I don't think Dad has the kind of money that inspires that kind of behavior," Jimmy quipped.

"She looks like a hippie in her picture," Jenny continued. "She's got to be with a name like that. And she's from Denver. She probably smokes weed!"

Jimmy made a fake shocked face and placed his hand on his heart as if he was having a heart attack. She reached over and punched his shoulder in protest. He pretended to fall into the passenger side door in great pain.

"Stop it, I'm being serious," she said.

"You're being insane," Jimmy replied as he straightened in his seat.

"This whole thing is insane. I don't know why I agreed to come. It's bad enough that Mom is gone, but now we have to be nice to Love," she said the name with a slight sneer. "And Dad said she invited some neighbor of hers or something?"

Jimmy nodded, "Yeah, Erin I think he said. Must be some hippie friend of hers. They're probably gonna smoke weed then eat all of the pies."

Jenny chuckled at the thought.

Jimmy patted her knee. "I know it's insane, little sister, but any Thanksgiving without Mom is always going to suck. We'll just have to do our best to get through it for Dad's sake."

Jenny nodded. He was right. He was usually right, a fact she'd refused to admit when they were younger.

"Now," Jimmy continued, "Can we get back to talking about my problems?"

"Yes." It was Jenny's turn to pat his knee.

Her heart hurt for her big brother. He and his husband, Paul, had only been separated for six weeks. Their 5-year old daughter, Penelope, was spending Thanksgiving with Paul and his family in Chicago. She'd seen the strain on Jimmy's face the moment he'd opened the door to her this morning.

Her brother had a slight build, average round facial features, fair skin that freckled easily, and reddish brown hair.

As siblings, they looked very much alike except her hair was a bit darker, even more so since she'd started coloring it a deeper auburn. His eyes were hazel and hers were brown. He was about 5'8" and she was 5'5". Those were the biggest differences between them, besides being different genders.

When she'd seen him this morning she noticed he was paler than usual, his eyes had the rimmed look of someone who had been crying. He was shaved and dressed nicely, which was normal, but she could tell he wasn't feeling himself. Who could be in his circumstances? A separation right before the holidays? Spending Thanksgiving without his little girl? He was probably in shock. She knew she was. The news of his and Paul's marital difficulties had come as a huge surprise to her. They'd always been the most solid couple she'd known, except for her parents of course.

"How are you doing?" Jenny asked, giving her brother a sympathetic look.

Jimmy sighed heavily. "The same as I was an hour ago."

"Aw, honey." Jenny patted his knee in empathy.

"It's all kind of surreal, you know?" Jimmy looked out over the picturesque landscape, his voice cracking a little as he spoke. "I mean it's so beautiful out here and it's going to be beautiful at the Lake House, and the holiday is happening even though Penny isn't here, and Paul isn't here...it just doesn't feel real."

Jenny watched her brother out of the corner of her eye as she maneuvered the car along the winding section of the road that took them into the wooded lake area, that much closer to their destination. Jimmy put his hands over his face, covering the fact that he was crying.

"Oh, honey," Jenny didn't know what else to say. She was no relationship expert and hadn't even known there was a problem between Jimmy and Paul until they separated. Her advice was next to useless.

"I just miss them so much." Jimmy wiped his eyes with a napkin from the pile they'd collected at the drive through getting their road trip breakfast.

"I know," Jenny replied. "Is there any way Paul would meet up with you the day after Thanksgiving? At least let Penny come for part of the holiday?" She thought having his daughter with him for a few days this week might help.

Jimmy shook his head 'no'. "We agreed that might be a lot of disruption for her, especially after all of the mayhem of him moving out."

Jenny nodded, "I can see that." She smiled at him encouragingly. "Well, we'll be there soon. You gonna call Penny when we get there?"

Jimmy nodded and they drifted into silence again, mesmerized by the scenery.

They had entered the woods and a myriad of brilliant fall colors blanketed the sky above the narrowing road. The ground under the trees was covered with crimson red, bright orange and deep golden leaves. All of them presumably fell from the branches above, but those branches looked dense with the same vibrant foliage. It seemed to Jenny that the trees couldn't possibly hold that many leaves. Yet there they were. Some of them were even falling lightly from the branches overhanging the road, floating downward on the breeze until her car drove through them scattering them in all directions.

"God it's gorgeous," Jimmy said out loud, echoing her sentiments.

Jenny pushed the button on her door so her window lowered and the cool autumn breeze filled the car. The air was damp with the scent of decomposing leaves, wood, and the rivers and lakes nearby.

The road curved and brought them to a new amazing view around each corner. Memories flooded her mind. Her parents had brought them here several times a year since she was small, five-years old to be exact. The drive was part of the experience and their Mom had always loved to see the fall colors.

"The bridge is next, right?" Jenny asked, pretty sure she knew where they were on the road.

Jimmy fumbled with his cell phone. "Slow down, I want to take a picture and send it to Paul...or Penny, I guess."

"Sure, we'll pull over."

As they came around the next curve the trees opened up, revealing a narrow river that snaked through the woods complete with an antique covered bridge to take them to the other side. There was a small shoulder right after the bend that allowed Jenny to pull her car over and park. They both got out, breathing in the wonderful smell of fall, enrapt with the scene.

"I can't get over the colors this year." Jimmy walked onto the blacktop, getting into a better position to take the picture.

Jenny could not have agreed more. She had always thought of the covered bridge as a kind of portal into the Lake House, which sat nestled in a grove of trees just five minutes up the road near a small lake.

She had crossed the covered bridge countless times over the years, beams of sunlight piercing through the narrow openings between the ancient wood planks, the bridge creaking under the weight of their car, the water tumbling over rocks below them in the river. Each time she made it to the other side Jenny always felt like she was transformed into something more, someone who belonged in the woods, was one with nature, a friend of the forest, maybe a magical fairy or woodland gnome. Silly, of course, but she still felt that way, even as a full grown woman who would be turning 33 in a few months.

Jenny felt a pang of grief as she realized, once again, that her mother wasn't waiting for her on the other side of the bridge. It didn't seem possible. Just like Jimmy said about Paul and Penny. The whole situation was surreal.

For a moment she let herself believe in the magic of the woods beyond the bridge. She wished as hard as she could that her mother would somehow still be alive on the other side, waiting for her with a huge smile and a warm hug, like always.

"Ready?" Jimmy asked. He'd finished taking pictures and rejoined her by the car.

She breathed in deep through her nose and exhaled through her mouth, then asked him, "Are you?"

Jimmy threw his arm over her shoulders and took in his own deep breath, then he wiggled her shoulders and gave her a big grin. "As ready as I'll ever be."

## 2

The first thing that jarred her was the sight of her father standing with his arm around the waist of a total stranger. Like a paper doll cut out had been slipped into place next to him where her mother would normally be standing–should be standing.

She had seen what his new wife looked like in the images he had emailed. They'd even managed to film a short video on his cell phone of their wedding, elopement really, that he'd sent to her and Jimmy. Her Dad had remarried on a fast informal trip to Vegas followed by a honeymoon in the Caribbean. Neither she nor Jimmy or anyone else had been invited. Not that Jenny would have gone.

The second thing Jenny noticed was the state of the woman standing next to her father. She was small, thin, and wearing a bright blue, high necked, shapeless dress that brushed against her ankles. The bright blue had a floral print of red poppies and pink roses, a garish contrast to the deep reds, golds and browns in the surrounding landscape.

Her hair was long, grey and soaking wet, sticking in messy strands against her cheeks and neck. Her feet were bare and must have been freezing as she stood with their father on the front porch, watching them get out of the car. The pictures and video could not have prepared Jenny for meeting the woman in the flesh. Nothing could have.

"Button!" Her Dad called from the porch as she shut the car door. "Jim Boy," he smiled widely at both of his children, his expression full of joyful anticipation.

Unable to wait for them to approach, their Dad, Rudy Combes, stepped down and walked towards them with open arms, leaving the woman behind, stranded on the porch by her bare feet.

Rudy was a small man, not much taller than Jenny and just a little shorter than his grown son. He had blue eyes, thinning white hair that had gotten thinner during their mother's long illness, and a strong round body. He was a retired electrician, a member of the United Methodist Church, a teller of lame jokes and a capable provider. He had worked hard his whole life, but never at the expense of his family. Her Dad had been home for dinner every night when they were growing up. He had been at every recital, school play, graduation, and wedding celebration. Well, Jimmy's wedding, not hers of course.

When her mother was diagnosed with cancer, her Dad took early retirement to care for her without complaint. And when she succumbed to that cancer two years later her Dad decided to donate his electrician talents to nonprofits and churches instead of returning to full time work. That's where he met his new wife, Love.

Love ran a nonprofit organization out of Denver that promoted art therapy for people, women mostly, who were healing from abusive relationships. All of this sounded great on paper, but it didn't keep Jenny from being full of uncertainty about the woman.

"Dad!" Jimmy reached him first and gave him a long hug.

Rudy gave him a few hard, emotional pats on the back. Jenny understood that her Dad was deeply concerned over his son's marital troubles and the gesture somehow conveyed that concern, making Jimmy tear up again.

"Jim Boy." Rudy pushed his son away and held him at arm's length, looking at him with worry and pain etched on his face. Then he pulled him in again for another bear hug. Jimmy laughed.

"Dad, you're choking me," Jimmy said, pulling away.

"How are you holding up?" Rudy asked, not letting him go until he got another good look at him.

"I'm all right." Jimmy gave a quick nod to his father, but his red rimmed eyes and strained expression didn't go unnoticed.

"Yes." Rudy nodded gruffly and squeezed Jimmy's shoulders. "You're gonna be fine, son. I'm glad you're here."

Jenny had positioned herself behind them, hiding from the smiling stranger marooned on the porch, wanting to greet her Dad before she was forced to meet his new wife. Rudy turned his attention to her, his face lighting up.

"Hi, Dad," Jenny said, stepping into his outstretched arms.

"Button," he said quietly into her ear as he squeezed her tight. The nickname settled in comfortably on her, making her feel safe and warm. When he was done with her big hug, he wrapped his arms around both her and Jimmy's waists and propelled them towards the porch. "Jenny, Jimmy, this is Love," he said.

Jenny could tell by his tone that her Dad was nothing but proud of Love. If he understood that she was anything but delighted to meet the woman who was now her stepmother, he didn't show it. He practically glowed with delight as he walked with them to where she stood. And Love, for her part, beamed back at him.

Love had a wide smile. Jenny was reminded of Julia Roberts, that kind of plain pretty face that didn't seem overly attractive until she lit up with a smile. Love was in her sixties at least and definitely not a movie star, but Jenny could see how she may have been quite beautiful when she was young. The blue dress, it turned out, was a vintage bathrobe and Love's bare feet were calloused along the sides of her big toes, suggesting she went barefoot a lot.

"It's so wonderful to finally meet you both," Love gushed a little, unable to contain her excitement.

Jenny leaned in when Love reached for her, allowing a short stiff hug. Love smelled like cinnamon, her wet hair giving off the aroma of a natural foods store. She was shorter than Jenny, making her the smallest among them.

Jenny stepped back awkwardly to allow Love a chance to hug Jimmy as well. Her cheeks hurt from smiling, but she didn't stop. She knew her Dad was watching.

"Let's go inside." Rudy said and opened the front door, ushering them all inside.

The warm smells of the Lake House surrounded her. Wide planked oak floors and high rough wood beamed ceilings welcomed her, making her feel like she had stepped back in time. Comfortable, worn furniture and handwoven rugs her parents had furnished the house with were the same as always. Even her mother's black and white checkered throw was tossed on the chair in the corner of the sitting room, as if she'd just gotten up to greet them when they arrived and left it there.

Jenny had not been back to the Lake House since her mother passed away. They hadn't had the heart as a family to do much over the holidays after her death. Jimmy and Paul had hosted Thanksgiving that year and they had all gone to spend Christmas at their parent's home in the suburbs with their Dad instead of making the trip to the lake country.

Jenny had always known returning would be difficult. She'd just never expected to be returning with a stepmother in the mix.

"Did you enjoy your drive?" Love asked as she motioned them past the front sitting room towards the kitchen, that faint smell of cinnamon, herbs and candles trailing behind her. "Aren't the trees absolutely beautiful? We've got some coffee on," Love kept chattering, perhaps from nerves, as she led them into the kitchen where the rough wooden beams and plank floors continued from the living room. Rudy followed them from the rear, herding them all into what had always been the best part of the Lake House.

The kitchen and dining room were one large space, full of light from rows of windows and a set of French doors on the outside wall. The large room had been remodeled years before in a traditional style.

The cabinets were off white, the counter tops were black as were the iron hinges, drawer and cabinet handles, and light fixtures. The inside wall was exposed brick with built in cubby holes to hold a variety of items including firewood for the large fireplace that sat at the end of the long room. The view out of the windows was remarkable. A brick patio just outside of the French doors ended at a short grass yard that led up to a thick grove of trees, gracing them today with the full range of fall colors.

"Sit down," Rudy told them as he and Love gathered mugs and small plates.

The smell of fresh coffee warmed the air and something else, a yeasty, cinnamon scent that got stronger as Love set a plate of fresh baked cinnamon rolls on the table. Rudy placed one mug in front of each of them and then fetched the pot of hot coffee and began pouring. Jenny looked across the long dining room table at Jimmy and wondered if he was thinking the same thing she was, their Dad had never served them coffee, ever. Jimmy caught her gaze and read the confusion in it, giving her an almost imperceptible shrug to let her know he noticed and he was going with the flow.

"I was hoping you would get here before your Dad ate all of the treats," Love said with a wide smile at Rudy.

"I just had to taste one to make sure it was baked through," Rudy answered, chuckling as he said it, his eyes twinkling.

Jenny cringed. Were they going to be flirting like this the whole week?

"They smell delicious." Jimmy took one of the gooey treats and plopped it onto the plate Rudy had set in front of him. He handed Jenny the serving spatula with a 'be nice' look.

"Yes, thank you," she managed to say.

She took a cinnamon roll even though she knew she wasn't going to be able to eat it. Her stomach was tight. She felt like a stranger in their Lake House, in her Mom's kitchen. Love playing hostess was too much. Jenny realized that she may not be able to eat anything for the entire Thanksgiving holiday.

"I'll just have one more," Rudy announced. Love shook her head and smiled at him. "They're too good!" He declared as he pulled a corner off and popped it in his mouth. "Besides, I burned up the first one in the hot tub."

Jimmy swallowed what was in his mouth and asked, "Hot tub?"

"Oh, honey," Love said to Rudy. "You let the cat out of the bag!"

"There goes the surprise!" Rudy threw up his hands in mock despair.

"What hot tub?" Jenny asked stiffly.

"It's an early Christmas present," Rudy explained. "I'll show you."

Sure enough, just outside the French doors and to the right, out of sight of the kitchen windows, sat an oversized, bubbling, completely gaudy hot tub.

"Did you bring a suit?" Rudy asked. Both Jenny and Jimmy shook their heads 'no'.

"Oh no, we should have told you to bring one." Love's face fell.

"Naw," Rudy waved his hand dismissively. "They both have so many suits packed away in this house. You'll find one that fits, don't you think?" He looked at them hopefully.

Jenny was still speechless. She was just trying to keep her mouth from dropping open. She looked to Jimmy to answer.

"Yeah, there are probably a few bathing suits here," Jimmy answered, but was a little distracted, still surprised at the appearance of such a modern, opulent amenity in their back yard. "Dad, what made you decide to do this?"

Rudy put his arm around Love's waist and looked at her happily. "I decided there's no time like the present."

Jenny cringed again. This was going to be a very long week.

LATER, in her room, Jenny was glad to be alone. The sun had set, Jimmy was in his room talking to Penny on the phone and, she hoped, Paul. Her Dad and Love were putting away dinner dishes. Jenny hadn't eaten much and excused herself to her room fairly early feigning fatigue. That wasn't a total lie.

She flopped onto her double bed that still had the rosebud patterned comforter she and her Mom had picked out. They had redecorated the room together when Jenny graduated from high school. At the time the rosebud pattern had seemed quite grown up.

She was tired. Getting up early, the long drive, her heart

aching for Jimmy and his separation, the newness of Love being here, the look of joy on her Dad's face, everything was too much. Hot tears filled Jenny's eyes and her heart sank.

She wished her Mom was here. That was the real drain, the real sorrow.

Jenny pushed the palms of her hands onto her eyes and pressed the tears out, wiping them away and sniffing hard. She had cried so much already. The air in her room hung around her, empty, joyless.

She rolled over so that she was on her side, the soft rosebud covered pillow under her head. Facing the window, more memories flooded her mind. She and her Mom had bought the white lace material for her curtains in town. Then her Mom had sewn them on her portable sewing machine, the one she kept in the basement laundry room. It had taken her less than an hour.

More tears rolled down Jenny's cheeks. She didn't try to stop them this time.

After a while the tears subsided and she sat up, wiping her face with the cuffs of her shirt. May as well get into her pajamas and go to bed. She couldn't make herself go downstairs and spend time with the newlyweds.

After all of her clothes were unpacked, she changed into her navy blue flannel jammies with the large, white polka dots. Pajamas were the one place where Jenny allowed her tight control of fashion to loosen up a little. She sat on the edge of her bed, wondering if she should just turn off the lamp and go to sleep or read a little bit first, when a stack of books on the small writing desk at her window caught her attention.

Jenny went to the desk and turned on the reading lamp that sat on its corner. A card lay on top of the stack. The image on the front of the card was a beautiful drawing of a peacock, its colors vibrant, the magnificent feathers on its tail embellished with swirls of gold, silver and purple glitter. Jenny picked up the card and flipped it open, recognizing the tilted flourish of her mother's cursive handwriting immediately.

Her hands trembled slightly. Jenny sat down at the small desk chair to read the message. It took her five tries before she could read through to the end without being blinded by tears.

*My Dearest Girl,*

*My Jennifer. I just watched you drive away, heading back to your life once again, looking so grown up and beautiful. It was wonderful to spend time with you this long weekend. Your father and I love it when you kids can make it out to see us. It can get a little quiet without you all around, and we didn't buy the Lake House to be quiet!*

*I remembered after you left that I forgot to tell you I found these old journals of yours when I was cleaning out some boxes. I am leaving them here on your desk so you'll be sure to see them when you come back next time.*

*I have to confess that I read through some of them. They're not diary journals, but story journals. So I thought maybe that wasn't too nosy of me.*

*You know what, Jenny? These stories are really, really good! You have always had a real talent for writing. I know you write a lot for your work, but can I be a pushy kind of Mom for a moment and suggest that maybe you should do more creative writing? It's just a thought. I would love to read more of your stories.*

*Well, I'm running out of room on this card. Isn't it pretty? I got it at that new little boutique by the sandwich shop. I'll take you there sometime when we're all here again. Won't that be fun?*

*Love you,*
*Mom*

When was this written? She flipped the card over and looked for a date. There was none. She thought back, trying to remember the last time she'd been to the Lake House. It was after her Mom got sick, she knew that for sure. But it must have been before they all realized how sick she really was.

Jenny ran her thumb over the handwriting and took in a shuddering breath. She should have come to see her parents every weekend. She shouldn't have assumed her Mom would be there forever.

Jenny closed the card and placed it carefully on the desk. She ran her hand over the pile of journals and spiral notebooks. The whole stack fit neatly on her nightstand and she had just enough room to set the peacock card up where she could see it from her pillow. She was about to pick up the top journal when she was interrupted by a soft knock on her door.

"Yes?" Jenny said.

The door swung open partway and Jimmy stuck his head in. "Are you still up?"

Jenny scooted over on her bed so there was enough room for him and patted the space next to her. He closed the door behind him and hopped onto her bed, stretching out next to her under the comforter and angling himself so their bodies were separate, but their heads slightly touched.

"How'd your phone call go?" she asked.

"Pretty awful." He sounded tired.

"I'm sorry." She reached for his hand and squeezed it. He squeezed back.

"It is what it is, you know?" he responded.

"Mmhmm," Jenny mumbled.

They were quiet for a few minutes, just staring at the light fixture above them, thinking. Jimmy finally broke the silence with a question, "So, what do you think of Love?"

Jenny didn't answer. She had already fallen asleep.

## 3

Warm smells of coffee brewing and bacon frying drifted upstairs, drawing Jenny out of bed and down the old staircase towards the kitchen. The ancient wooden steps creaked under her pink fuzzy slippers and she pulled the matching pink robe more snugly around her in the chilly morning air.

The Lake House had been built in the early 1800's. A Cape Cod style, solid and dependable, but definitely prone to uneven temperatures throughout. The upstairs hall and bathroom, the stairway and the front sitting room were almost always colder than the rest of the house. Jenny didn't mind. It made her feel like she was on vacation. She followed her nose into the toasty kitchen where she found her Dad cooking breakfast with Love.

"Good morning, Button!" He smiled at her and lifted an empty mug in the air. "Do you want some coffee? We just made a fresh pot."

"Yes, thank you," she mumbled, still groggy as she perched on one of the tall kitchen stools

"Cream and sugar, right?" Love asked, setting the small

cream pitcher and sugar bowl in front of Jenny, anticipating a 'yes' response.

Jenny nodded. "Thanks."

Love looked decidedly more put together this morning. She was fully dressed, wearing jeans that were worn, but not full of holes or anything. She had a lavender Henley shirt on under a long pastel striped sweater whose sleeves reached all the way over the palms of her hands. When Love's hair was dry, Jenny noted, it was a pretty silver color and naturally wavy. It fell past her shoulders which didn't quite make her look like a witch, as Jenny might have thought it would, but more like an old wise woman from a fantasy story.

Classical music played on the small CD/Radio combo that sat on the counter. Jenny watched as her father tended to the bacon that popped and sizzled in a large cast iron skillet and Love slid a casserole dish full of what looked like French toast into the oven.

"Did you sleep well?" he asked as he repositioned himself so Love could place another skillet on the burner next to the one occupied by bacon. Love kept her hand on her Dad's back just a few moments longer than necessary as she moved behind him to go to the refrigerator.

"Yes, I did," she managed to answer.

"Is that bacon or am I still dreaming?" Jimmy announced his arrival with the question. He staggered into the kitchen in a kind of fake sleepwalk routine, bundled in his own warm robe, but without the fuzzy slippers.

"Coffee, son?" Rudy held up another empty mug. Jimmy nodded and sat on the stool next to Jenny.

They sipped their coffee and observed their Dad in the kitchen with Love. With sideways glances, Jenny watched as Jimmy emerged from his sleepy cocoon and the strangeness of their Dad's behavior registered with him. When Rudy pulled a bag of oranges out of the refrigerator and started slicing them in half in order to juice them with a small, hand held juicer, Jenny and Jimmy shared a look of disbelief.

"Dad, I've never seen you cook before," Jenny said.

"I like to cook," he answered, happily grinding the pulpy juice from an innocent orange rind. "I guess I never had time when you were growing up. I was working all the time."

"We're making a big breakfast today. My friend, Aaron, is coming this morning," Love interjected.

Right. The little old lady who smokes weed.

"Where do you know Erin from?" Jimmy asked.

"Oh, wow." Love stopped what she was doing, which was apparently hand whipping sugared cream cheese with some blueberries. "We've been neighbors in Denver for more than 30 years now."

"How nice," Jenny said, imagining Love and another quirky free spirited little old lady in their back yard full of rose bushes and bird baths, smoking a joint. She gave Jimmy an amused look and knew by his quick nod that he was thinking something similar.

"I'm excited for you both to meet Aaron," Love continued. "I think you'll all get along wonderfully." She flashed her brilliant smile at them, which was a little overwhelming first thing this morning.

"I'm sure we will," Jenny answered politely. Internally she sighed, another stranger she had to be nice to over Thanksgiving.

"Can we help you with anything?" Jimmy asked, always congenial.

The siblings were given the task of setting the dining room table. They used the casual off-white stoneware with the embossed edges and plain off-white cloth napkins. Love suggested they set a place for her soon to arrive buddy, so they put two places on what had always been Jenny's side of the table.

Once everything was ready the kitchen seemed even more warm and inviting and Jenny decided she could probably make small talk if necessary, as long as she had plenty of coffee. She thought briefly about going upstairs to change out of her polka dot pajamas, but decided there was no need. How important was it to look good for Love's little old lady friend?

All of the delicious food filled the center of the table, smelling wonderful. They pulled their chairs out and sat down at their places to dig in. The sound of crunching gravel in the driveway sent Love into a flurry of activity.

"Aaron's here!" She exclaimed, popping out of her chair and flying by them on her way to the front door. "This is going to be such fun!"

Rudy watched her excitement with much pleasure. Jenny saw the gleam of satisfaction in his eyes as his new wife hurried to meet her friend and she felt a sense of betrayal. It didn't seem right that he could look at another woman that way. Rudy's gaze turned to Jenny and she dropped hers to the floor, hoping she didn't have a scowl on her face.

"Have you met Erin?" Jimmy asked.

Rudy nodded. "He's very nice."

He?

Jimmy and Jenny barely had a moment to exchange surprised looks before a tall, handsome, young man entered the kitchen followed by Love. They all stood up to greet him.

"Aaron, nice to see you again." Rudy stuck out his hand.

"You too, Rudy." Aaron took his hand and shook it firmly. "Thanks again for inviting me." He turned his attention towards the siblings and Jenny, for one, was at a loss for words.

Aaron was tall, at least 6'1", ruggedly built, with long, wavy blonde hair loosely pulled into a man bun. His features were strong and sharp like a Viking's, and his eyes were such a bright, frosty blue they almost glowed. He had a lengthy rough beard of blonde and red whiskers that Jenny at once hated and found attractive. His skin was tanned with that reddish tone that the fair skinned are cursed. He wore a navy blue, long sleeved T-shirt, worn jeans and a pair of broke in brown hiking boots.

He looked like he knew how to build a wooden boat from scratch. He looked like he had just cross country skied into a snowed in village to deliver medicine to sick children. He looked like he could brew his own pale ale while gutting a fish and playing the fiddle. He definitely did not look like a little old lady.

Aaron locked his eyes onto hers and a flutter of nerves burst through her stomach. She couldn't think of one thing to say to this man. His icy blue eyes seemed to be holding her in a trance.

Time froze for a moment as they connected, albeit silently. His eyes searched hers until he found something, what was it? Pain? Loneliness? Attraction? Jenny's feelings were in a free fall. She couldn't put her finger on what was happening between them, but she could tell the moment Aaron found what he was seeking, because she was suddenly exposed, vulnerable, and had the insane desire to flee out the French doors.

Then it was gone. The bright light of his searching gaze dimmed. He toned it down. She understood immediately that he had seen into her for the briefest second, felt her discomfort, and pulled back. Like a horse whisperer or a psychiatrist working with frightened children, he knew when to back off, but her heart had quickened nevertheless. It still beat loudly in her chest.

"Hello." Aaron's face broke into a smile that crinkled the corners of his eyes. Eyes that twinkled so brightly it was difficult for Jenny to maintain her gaze. She fought the urge to look away.

"Hello," Jimmy answered, thankfully one of them could speak. "I'm Jimmy."

Aaron stepped towards him and they shook hands, Jimmy smiling just a smidge too hard. Jenny stifled a giggle. She knew Aaron's intense good looks were not lost on her brother.

Aaron turned towards her, causing nervous butterflies in her stomach again. The urge to giggle grew stronger. Jimmy slipped behind Aaron and peered at her over the taller man's shoulder, his eyes wide with an 'Oh My God He's Gorgeous' look. Jenny had to completely ignore him and focus hard on greeting Love's friend appropriately. That didn't work.

"I thought you were a woman," she said, startled at the words as soon as they left her mouth. Aaron's smile went from welcoming to politely confused. Jimmy disappeared behind Aaron's back, she was getting no help from him. She tried to explain, "I mean, my middle name's Erin with an 'e' and, you know..." she fanned her hand back and forth between them, "Aaron...Erin...I thought Aaron was a girl's name." Without thinking, she allowed her fingertips to touch his chest and felt the muscles underneath his shirt for a brief, enticing moment. "So I thought you were a girl!" A nervous laugh escaped her lips.

She wrapped her arms around her waist in a self-hug and was immediately reminded that she had on her polka dot pajamas and pink robe, and still had a head full of bed hair. Oh my God, had she really just touched his chest?

The whole room was silent. Aaron hadn't looked away from her since she started her awkward ramble. Jenny heard Jimmy clear his throat from somewhere on the other side of this rather marvelous looking man. She knew her brother was fighting not to laugh. Her own desire to giggle abandoned her completely and heat rose in her cheeks. Aaron's brilliant, icy eyes searched hers again, this time they were full of humor. He cocked his head towards hers in a charming nod.

"Sorry to disappoint," he grinned, expertly converting this awkward interaction into a playful moment. Their first private joke.

She blushed even harder, ducking her head and smiling at the floor in an uncontrollable coy reaction. As she lifted her gaze she saw her Dad and Love watching them with blatant knowing smiles plastered across their faces. The soft, squishiness she'd been feeling suddenly hardened. Why were they looking at her like that? Were they trying to set her up with this man bunned hipster? Was Love playing matchmaker?

Jenny stiffened. She dropped her gaze to the table and sat back down in her chair, shrugging nonchalantly to indicate she was not disappointed. Why would she care either way? If he was a man or a woman or an orangutan, it didn't matter to her. He was just another stranger in her mother's house for Thanksgiving and that's how she would treat him.

## 4

The first item on the agenda after cleaning up breakfast dishes was horseshoes. At least, that was the first item on Rudy's agenda. Jenny had helped clear the table, taken the cloth napkins downstairs to the laundry and upon returning found that Love and Aaron had taken over washing and drying dishes.

"Your Dad and Jimmy went out to play horseshoes," Love told her. "We've got the rest of this I think, don't we?" She looked up at Aaron, because everyone in the house had to look up when speaking to him, they were a tiny lot and he was like a great, blonde lumberjack among them.

"Absolutely," he responded. "We can catch up on old times." Aaron nudged Love with his elbow and it was all Jenny could do to keep from rolling her eyes. She managed not to, excusing herself to go get dressed instead.

She took a quick shower in the small upstairs bath and spent another half hour drying her hair and putting on a little makeup. She didn't want to get too fixed up, but after this morning she felt like putting her best face forward, so to speak.

Once back in her room she sat down at her desk. She could see her Dad and Jimmy in the back yard playing horse-shoes. They were chatting and laughing with each other and she watched them for a while. She was lucky to have both of them in her life. They were good men, she knew that for sure. Other men in her life had not turned out to be quite as supportive or loyal or even as much fun as her Dad and brother. Sometimes she wondered if they'd spoiled her for any kind of romantic relationship. She hadn't found a man that lived up to her expectations yet. Maybe she never would.

"You'll find the right man one day," her mother used to tell her when Jenny was having one of her lonely breakdowns. "Don't settle for the wrong one. You deserve to find real love." Jenny remembered those talks fondly. They would have cake and hot tea with honey if it was cold outside, or cookies and iced tea if it was hot. Their conversations about boys and romance were never contained to only one part of the year.

Jenny sighed. She looked at the journals and card resting on her nightstand and decided she would spend some quiet time in her room reading her old stories. She brought every-thing back to her desk and turned on the little lamp. After reading through the peacock card again, she propped it up on the corner of the small desk where she could see it, then picked up one of the oldest journals and flipped it open.

The first story was about a circus elephant who escapes during a show and rampages through the streets, ultimately being trapped and killed for rebelling against its captors. The last chapter was particularly gory, the elephant dying in a huge pool of blood still wearing its gaudy circus hat. Dark. That was from her middle school years. The writing was juve-nile, but really not too bad for a 13 or 14-year old girl, she thought.

She picked up the next journal and skimmed through it, looking for something she'd written in high school. She found one with the title scrawled in her wide, optimistic teenage cursive across the top, "Once I Loved You". Reading through the story, Jenny recalled the boy it was based on, a beautiful dark haired quiet boy who'd been one of the nice popular kids. He was a star on the baseball team and Jenny had developed a real interest in baseball while suffering under that crush. The main character in the book was named after him, Gabe. She smiled at the memory. The interest in Gabe had faded after she wrote this story, as had her interest in baseball.

She looked through each of the journals. As a child she'd always wanted to be a writer. She'd never told anyone, but she was pretty sure her mother had guessed. Intimidated by the brilliant literary writers she admired, Jenny had chosen to pursue a degree in Communications rather than English. She'd worked in the Communications department of a healthcare company for the last six years. They operated several hospitals and it was her responsibility to keep up the internal communication between management and staff, mostly through informational emails, newsletters and presentations at large meetings. The job suited her and provided her the opportunity to use some of her writing skills, but it was nothing like writing fiction.

The last journal in the pile was different than the others. Instead of the used look and the general teenage girl designs of the previous covers, lots of pinks and purples and bubble letters, this one was a sleek deep green with gold script lettering on the front that read 'Dream Big, Be Brave.' And it was brand new. Jenny opened it to find that it was empty save for an inscription on the inside front cover from her Mom.

*Jenny, For all of your new stories! Love, Mom*

She didn't want to cry again, but she did. Just a little. Just enough to mess up her makeup.

"Jenny." A knock sounded at the same time Jimmy opened the door and popped his head into her room. His expression fell when he saw her. "You're still in your robe?"

"Do you mind?" Jenny pulled her robe tighter around her.

"Dad wants to have a ping pong tournament. Love's making snacks."

"Snacks? We just ate."

"It's been, you know, an hour since then." Jimmy grinned at her. "I guess Aaron brought some stuff. Apparently he works at a natural food company and is some kind of foodie." He paused, then wiggled his eyebrows up and down at her. "In addition to being the hottest human being I've seen in a very, very long time!"

"Shut up," Jenny said, trying not to laugh.

Jimmy did a silly swing walk over to where she sat and grabbed her by the arms, standing her up as he did. He made a pleading face, "Come on! You can't just mope up here in your room forever. Put on something fabulous and get downstairs to play some highly competitive ping pong with that gorgeous man."

Jenny laughed, "He's not that gorgeous."

"Right, Miss Melt Into a Puddle of Goo when you met him." Jimmy let go of her in mock disgust. "If I was single and he was gay there would be no holding me back."

"You're sure he's not gay?" She asked.

"I'm sure," Jimmy sighed, a sound of resignation. "Besides, I'm still officially married, so even if he was..." He let the rest of his sentence trail off into sadness.

"Oh, honey." Jenny reached out to give him a comforting hug.

"Nope." He held her at arm's length. "I'm not doing sad today. We've got horseshoes, we've got ping pong, we've got a hunk waiting for us in the basement, and enough food to choke an elephant. Today is going to be fun, dammit!"

Jenny agreed to join the ping pong tournament and sent Jimmy out of the room so she could get dressed. She chose a pair of jeans and a dark grey blouse with a crisscross V-neck that hung nicely around her shape without being too clingy. She slipped on socks and a pair of flat tennis shoes, more to keep her feet warm than anything, and made her way down to the basement.

The merriment could be heard before she even reached the main floor, which was empty because everyone had already moved to the basement. The house smelled delicious, she assumed from whatever snacks had been prepared. Jenny walked quickly by the empty sitting room where her Mom used to sit in the chair in the corner, reading. She knew that if her Mom was alive she would probably have spent the morning visiting with her in that room, but she didn't want to think about that too much right now.

The basement was a fun recreation space. It was all one great room except for a storage area, a bathroom and the laundry room. A giant sectional sofa with a big screen TV took up one side of the room. They had spent countless hours watching movies on that TV as kids. Right now it was tuned to a football game, it looked like college teams. The other side of the room had a small bar with a short counter, which currently held three trays of hors devours and a pitcher full of sliced citrus fruit floating in a dark red liquid. That side of the room also held a juke box, a fuzball table and, Rudy's all-time favorite, a ping pong table, where he now dominated one side of what appeared to be a heated volley with Aaron.

Love and Jimmy were perched on two of the three barstools that bumped up against the bar. Love gave Jenny a happy little wave when she entered the room. Jenny returned it with a conservative smile.

"This looks serious," Jenny said as she approached the table.

"You're up next," Jimmy told her.

"I've already lost," Love said brightly, scooting out the empty barstool next to her so Jenny could sit down. With no other options, Jenny took the seat. She positioned herself so her back was towards the bar so she could watch the action.

"Sangria?" Love asked, moving the pitcher towards her.

Jenny sipped Sangria and took in the sight of her elderly father whipping a much younger man in ping pong. It wasn't that Aaron was bad at the game. It's just that her Dad was so good at it. Her vantage point made it easy for her to appreciate Aaron's physical attributes while not appearing to stare. She liked how he talked and laughed with her Dad, and she even liked how his hair got a little tussled from the exertion, long pieces of it falling down into his angular features. She wondered how long his hair actually was and what he looked like when it was down. Once or twice, he glanced in her direction and she sucked in her breath. The piercing, cold blue of his eyes riveted her attention in those moments and she couldn't look away.

"You're up, Button," Rudy exclaimed the instant Aaron missed the final point. He turned and pointed at her with his paddle, his face alight with the thrill of victory. Aaron placed his hands on the table and feigned exhaustion. Jenny popped a mini mushroom quiche into her mouth and hopped off of the barstool to take his place.

"This is a mean game," Aaron said as he handed her the paddle. Their hands brushed against each other in the exchange and once again Jenny felt the warmth of him tingle through her fingertips.

"Only with my Dad," she said, trying not to smile too much at him, and failing.

"Have you seen the Bruce Lee video when he plays ping pong with nunchucks?" Jimmy piped up from the bar.

"Yes!" Aaron exclaimed. He mimed nunchuck moves as he approached the bar and he and Jimmy entered into a lively conversation about Bruce Lee and Kung Fu movies.

"Ready?" Rudy asked Jenny. She nodded and the game was on.

Jenny wasn't as good at ping pong as her Dad, but she was close. Countless ping pong tournaments had occurred in this basement since she was a little girl. Both she and Jimmy had learned early that their Dad wasn't going to just let them win. They had practiced with each other and eventually become real competition for their table tennis obsessed father.

Her Dad delighted in her expertise as they served and volleyed and teased each other good naturedly. Despite her best efforts, Jenny finally succumbed to his lightening reflexes and lost the game, allowing Jimmy to take his place as the next challenger.

Jenny took a seat at the empty bar stool between Aaron and Love, the latter immediately offered her a raspberry filled doughnut hole.

"No, thanks," Jenny said. "They look delicious, though. Did you make them?"

"Aaron brought them," Love replied.

"Did you make them?" Jenny asked Aaron, glad to have even the tiniest subject to build a polite conversation with both of them.

Aaron shook his head 'no'. "I brought them from a little store near my house."

"Barnaby's?" Love asked with delight.

"Yep," he answered as he took the tray Love offered him and ate one of the doughnut holes.

"So, you two lived next to each other?" Jenny thought she should at least try to put the pieces together.

"Yes," Love answered. "Aaron's parents moved next door when you were, what, two or three?" She looked at Aaron for confirmation.

Aaron nodded as he took a drink of his Sangria. Jenny tried not to notice the way his neck muscles flexed when he swallowed.

"That's what I'm told," he answered.

"We, my husband and I, had a dog named Pewter. A little silver haired terrier," Love explained. "And that dog loved Aaron from the moment they met. They were like best friends growing up together." She gave Aaron a sweet smile, which he returned.

"Love was my second Mom when I was a kid," Aaron said. "Still is."

Jenny had a sudden urge to leave the room. She stayed seated, however, she didn't want to seem bothered. She wanted to remain cool and aloof and unruffled.

Aaron leaned in towards her, his eyes smiling at the corners. "You are an excellent ping pong player."

A small, almost imperceptible, shiver ran down her spine. She could feel her heart beating a little faster than normal. Was she really that affected by his physical presence? Ridiculous. It was probably the alcohol in the drink. Sangria was always stronger than you thought it was going to be. She took in a deep breath to calm herself and realized he was so close she could smell him. He smelled like soap and fresh cut wood and leather. Jenny inhaled again without thinking, liking his smell, then realized he was waiting for her to respond.

"Oh, yeah, Dad insisted we play with him. It's a tradition at the Lake House."

Aaron nodded with appreciation. "That's nice. This is a beautiful house, too."

"Isn't it?" Love chimed in, looking around the basement recreation space with admiration. "I've been in love with it since we got here."

"Yes," Jenny said quickly, not hearing the spite until it was out of her mouth. "Mom and Dad did a really great job fixing it up."

The air around the three of them grew quiet, even as Rudy and Jimmy continued with their raucous game a few feet away. Jenny's throat felt tight and she stared into her glass of Sangria without looking up. She didn't need to look up to feel the tension from her remark. The hurt. Inwardly she was defiant, stamping her feet at Love and all that her presence at the Lake House represented, like a little girl who wasn't getting her way. She was also ashamed. Sorry that she couldn't reciprocate the kindness Love seemed to be trying to show her and guilty for resenting her Dad's newfound happiness. The Sangria in her glass blurred and Jenny was mortified to realize she was about to cry.

"Excuse me," she muttered, taking her drink and hurrying away from the bar and up the stairs.

## 5

The next day was Sunday. Jenny got up before sunrise, dressed in warm layers including her favorite oversized navy blue sweater, slipped the green journal and a pen into her sweater pocket and went carefully down the old stairs to try and keep them from creaking. At the bottom of the stairs she quietly opened the closet and retrieved her coat and hat. Aaron was sleeping on an air mattress set up in the front sitting room, since all three bedrooms were already occupied. Jenny couldn't see him, but she could hear him breathing deeply like a sleeping bear. She snuck down the hallway and slipped out the French doors off the kitchen, just in time to see the first rays of morning light sparking through the trees.

It was cold. Really cold. Jenny half wished she'd brought gloves on top of her hat and coat, but didn't want to go back inside and risk running into anyone. She wanted this day to start off clear, no botched conversations, no coming upon Love somewhere she expected to see her mother, nothing but her and the trees and the crisp, cold autumn air.

She strolled past the giant Oak tree in the side yard, where their tire swing still hung invitingly. She considered it for a moment. No, too cold. Jenny shoved her bare hands in her coat pockets and followed a small path into the woods that led to the clearing. By the time she got there the sun was halfway up. Dawn painted the trees and leaves with a golden glow and Jenny heard geese honking as they flew overhead.

She paused for a moment at the edge of the clearing and took in its pure beauty. The clearing was just that, about an acre of cleared area hidden in the dense woods on their property. It was covered in a carpet of thick grass with various flowers and shrubs, both wild and perennials that she and her mother had planted over the years, growing around the edges, some reaching into the grassy areas. There were two benches in the clearing. One on the east side facing west and one on the west side facing east. They'd placed them this way so they could come in the morning and watch the sun rise over the trees or the evening and watch it set on the other side.

Jenny sat down in the east facing bench. The wood was so cold it almost felt wet through her clothes, but there had been neither rain nor frost overnight. She took in a deep breath of the sharp morning air, the scent of ancient trees and rich soil filling her lungs. She wished she had a thermos of coffee or, better yet, hot chocolate. Her Mom had always brought hot chocolate in their huge thermos with the red plaid print on the outside when it was cold. She had decided to skip making coffee before coming out this morning, she figured just the smell could wake someone up, especially Aaron since he was sleeping in the room right next to the kitchen.

The geese sounded again, followed by the chirping of other birds that Jenny didn't know well enough to name. Soon they would be flitting through the trees and in and out of the shrubbery looking for bright red berries or seeds to eat. The clearing was secluded enough that there was usually no noise from any of their nearest neighbors and literally none from any cars driving on the nearest roads. Jenny relished the silence. She spread her arms across the back of the bench and kicked her booted feet out in front of her, crossing them at the heels. The rays of the sun were bright enough now that she could feel them warming her cheeks. She gave a contented sigh. She would sit here and let the sun do its work until the air lost its bite, then she would do what she came here for, she would write.

Reading through her old stories had sparked something inside of her, something that had been sleeping for a long time. The message from her Mom had brought it all to the surface and Jenny felt like she at least owed her Mom the respect to consider her suggestion to do more creative writing. So she sat in the chilly morning until it wasn't so chilly anymore, then she pulled the green journal and pen from her sweater pocket and positioned herself sideways on the bench so she could write comfortably.

She read the inscription again and smiled, then turned to the first, perfectly blank, empty page and stared. She hadn't given one thought yet towards what she actually wanted to write, and the blank page wasn't giving her any great ideas. She wrote the date on the top right hand side of the page and the pen wimped out halfway through the year. She shook it and tried again. She stuck the tip of the pen just inside her open mouth and breathed on it, maybe it was too cold for the ink to run. That worked and she was able to scribble the rest of the date, but then the pen just hung there over the starting point on the top left of the page. Nothing.

A heavy crunching sound echoed through the clearing and Jenny forgot all about her writing. The crunching was definitely steps of someone, or something, approaching. Her mind whirled with stories of bears in the woods and she cursed herself silently for not bringing her mace. She stood up to face where she thought the sound was coming from, the opening of the path into the clearing, which was less than ten feet from the bench. Whatever it was, it wasn't crashing through the trees but staying on the path and heading right towards her. Even if it was a deer, rutting season could still be affecting the bucks in the area and they might be dangerous. For an instant she thought she might duck into the trees behind the bench and hide, but that thought came too late, the culprit emerged from the path into the clearing at a full run.

It was Aaron.

Jenny yelped when she saw him, a visceral reaction that she couldn't control. Her hands flew to her mouth to cover it, making her drop the pen and journal on the ground.

Aaron's forward momentum was disrupted by the sight and sound of her. He did a cartoonish scrambling that propelled him backwards a few steps before his mind registered who she was and he stopped. He put his right hand over his heart and let out a surprised laugh.

"Jeez, Jenny!" He laughed again. His breathing was hard not only from the shock, but because he was out for what looked like a morning run. He wore dark grey sweat pants, a loose T-shirt and a faded red hooded sweatshirt. "You scared the hell out of me!"

Jenny dropped her hands from her mouth. "You, too!"

Aaron noticed the journal and pen on the ground and walked towards her. "I'm sorry, let me help you get these." She started to refuse, but he was already down on one knee in front of her picking up her items. He stood up and brushed a few stray leaves off of the journal before handing it and the pen back to her. "I didn't know anyone was out here."

"I came out here to..." she paused, not certain how to explain.

Aaron's eyes flicked to the journal in her hand then back up. "To write?"

Jenny nodded mutely. The morning glow tumbled through his hair, making it even more golden blonde. His beard looked lustrous with its red and gold highlights.

"Do you come out here to write every morning?" He asked.

"Yes, well, starting this morning."

"I'll have to take my run another way. I don't want to disturb you." He smiled at her. It was a gentle smile. Maybe it was because the morning was so beautiful, maybe being in the clearing made her feel calm and centered, she wasn't really sure what came over her, but what she blurted out next came as a surprise to both of them.

"Oh, no, it's no problem. Come here any time you want. My Mom and I used to come here all the time...with hot chocolate." She smiled a little nervously, unsure why she had shared that last bit with him.

Aaron shifted his weight from one foot to the other and considered her for a moment. Jenny felt exposed as he looked at her, but tried to return his gaze with equal calm. Once again she was under the spell of his crystal blue eyes, but she was able to let him look into her without panicking this time. He took his time, searching her eyes for what, she wasn't sure. The truth? Just when it was about to get uncomfortable, his face lit up with a big grin.

"That's very nice of you. I might do that when I'm done with my run."

"Good" She nodded, silently recognizing that she was disappointed he wasn't going to join her on the bench right now.

"I'll let you get back to your writing," he said as he took a few steps back towards the opening in the trees.

She gave him a little wave, then thought of something. "There's a path that starts near the mailbox in the driveway.

It goes all the way down to the covered bridge. If, you know, you're interested."

"Great! Thanks," he answered. He nodded at her then turned, his walk turning into a jog as he disappeared into the woods.

When Jenny got back to the house breakfast preparations were in full swing again. It wasn't quite as strange to see Love and her Dad cooking together this morning as it was yesterday. Maybe it was something that would grow on her over time. Aaron arrived, freshly showered after his run and smelling good.

"Good morning, again," he said, giving her a quick wink. A flurry of butterflies shimmered through her stomach. She shook them off.

"Again?" Rudy asked. She wondered if his Dad radar was turning on.

"We ran into each other outside this morning, in the clearing," she explained.

"Are you ready to make your world famous crepes?" Love asked Aaron, holding up a nonstick frying pan.

"Absolument!" Aaron answered in pretty good French. He took the pan from Love then stopped uncertainly, realizing that he was in a strange kitchen and didn't know where anything was kept.

"Jenny, would you mind showing him around the kitchen?" Love asked her. "We'll set the table." With that, Love led her Dad into the dining room.

Jenny was a little taken aback. It was the first time Love had spoken to her like that, like they were more than strangers, like they might be part of the same family. She didn't have much time to think about how strange it made her feel, because Aaron was still standing in the middle of the kitchen holding his frying pan.

Jenny showed him where the mixing bowls and utensils

were. Then she opened the fridge and pulled out the ingredients he requested. He didn't consult a list, but told her from memory. Soon she was leaning against the counter watching him mix the crepe batter with a wire whisk. Again, a few strands of blonde, wavy hair had come loose from his man-bun and fell lightly against his cheek, getting hung up with the whiskers of his beard. It took everything in Jenny not to reach out and tuck the stray pieces behind his ear. What was the matter with her? She should try and think of something to say instead.

"You speak French?" She asked.

"Yes," Aaron dipped his head in a half nod. "Well, je parle un peu français." He held his finger and thumb together indicating a tiny amount.

Jenny laughed and answered with a rusty accent, "Moi aussi, un peu."

"Excellent!" He exclaimed with the French pronunciation. "Did you learn in France?"

"Oh, no," Jenny shook her head, pooh-poohing the idea with a chuckle. "I took some in high school and one semester in college."

"You have a good accent," Aaron complimented as he threw a pat of butter in the pan that was heating on the stove. When the butter hit, it sizzled and slid around the surface. He tilted the pan until the butter had coated it, then poured a dipper full of the thin, yellow batter into the center. Immediately he moved the pan in a slow, swirling motion until the batter filled the bottom. He obviously had some skill in the kitchen.

"Did you learn to speak French in France?" She asked, curious.

"Yes, mostly." He picked up a flat spatula from the counter and talked as he watched the edges of the crepe turn dry and brown. "My parents and I spent a lot of time there when I was growing up. They're there now, in fact. With my father's family."

"Too bad you couldn't be with your parents on the holiday," Jenny offered.

Aaron lifted his shoulder and let it drop in an almost imperceptible shrug. "I didn't want to spend the whole week flying and getting jet lag. Besides," he looked into the dining area where Love was showing her Dad how to fold the cloth napkins properly, "It's great to spend some time with Love."

"Yeah," Jenny said, though she was looking at the floor. "That's great."

"So far, I've had a really good time," Aaron continued. When Jenny looked up he was grinning at her, his eyes twinkling. Her butterflies came back, but before she had a moment to squash them, Aaron turned his attention to the frying pan. He lifted the pan off of the flame, jiggled it forward and back a few times to loosen the crepe from the bottom, then flicked his wrist so the crepe let go, flew in the air, turned half over and landed back in the pan on its uncooked side. Jenny's eyes flew open with delight. Aaron gave her another wink. Show off.

"Did you learn to cook in France, too?" She asked with a laugh.

"Oui, mademoiselle." He placed the pan on the burner, let go of the handle and turned his palms upward, as if he'd just done a magic trick. "Voila!"

Despite her best efforts, Jenny's butterflies returned with a vengeance.

ॐ    6    ॐ

Jimmy finally made it downstairs when they were halfway through breakfast. He was dressed and chipper, but Jenny thought he looked like he hadn't slept much. During breakfast, he leaned into her ear and told her he'd been on the phone with Paul since five in the morning.

"Is that a good thing?" Jenny was hopeful.

"Maybe," he answered.

After breakfast was cleaned up, Rudy made an announcement.

"All right," he started, reaching his arm around Love's shoulders as he spoke. "This year is the first Thanksgiving we're hosting as a married couple." Love smiled up at him and the sight of it wrung Jenny's heart. "It's also the first big Thanksgiving plans we've had since your Mom passed away." He looked meaningfully at Jimmy and Jenny. "And, the first time most of us have had the pleasure of Aaron at our Thanksgiving table." He smiled at Aaron as he spoke. "Love and I were talking and we would like all of us to come together as a group, as a family, and create the Thanksgiving menu."

Jenny looked at Jimmy, confused. What was there to think about a Thanksgiving menu? It was turkey, stuffing, mashed potatoes, gravy and pumpkin pie. Boom, you're done.

"A menu?" Jimmy voiced the question for both of them.

"We want everyone to come up with two dishes. So one side dish and either an appetizer or a dessert. Then we're going to go to town together tomorrow and shop for ingredients so we can get cooking on Wednesday!" Rudy beamed at them, his arm still draped around Love. Her serene expression made it obvious she agreed with this plan, maybe she'd been the orchestrator of it from the beginning. "I understand Aaron is quite a cook, and we got a taste of that this morning with those crepes." Rudy rubbed his rounded belly, like he was a cartoon mayor of a cartoon town who'd just eaten a big meal.

"Rudy and I will manage the turkey, so you don't have to worry about that," Love spoke up.

Jenny scowled. This wasn't how they had ever done Thanksgiving.

"Those were good crepes," Jimmy said to Aaron, giving her a sideways glance. If nobody else could tell that she disliked this plan, she knew her brother could. Her Dad probably could, too, but he seemed to be perfectly comfortable telling her how it was going to be despite how it might make her feel.

"Sound good?" Rudy asked, making eye contact with Aaron, then Jimmy, then her. Both of the guys nodded in agreement, Aaron with more enthusiasm than she would have expected. When her Dad looked at her and waited for a response, Jenny couldn't get herself to say 'yes' or indicate her compliance in any manner whatsoever. A memory played on a loop in her mind. It was her Mom pulling the perfectly browned turkey out of the oven, moving it to its special platter and placing that platter on the table for carving. It had been the same year after year after year. She hadn't been expecting anything else. She didn't want anything else.

"Does that sound good, Button?"

Tears filled her eyes without warning. Her throat tightened, first with sorrow then with shame. She looked hard at the floor where her shoes blurred. She blinked and two fat tears fell towards the floor, splashing on top of each of her shoes. She shook her head up and down for 'yes'.

"Oh, sweetie." Love's voice sounded, kind and sympathetic.

"It's fine," Jenny blurted out. "I'm sorry. I'm fine and the menu thing is fine." That was all she could say. She turned and hurried up to her room without looking at any of them.

Once she'd cried out all of her tears, she still didn't feel like facing anyone. She laid on her bed for a while, thinking. She made a move to turn on her side and felt the uncomfortable lump of the green journal that was still stuck deep inside her sweater pocket. She sat up and took it out along with the pen and in a sudden flash of insight knew exactly what she wanted to write as her first entry. Sitting down at her desk, Jenny got busy putting down on paper all of her memories of her Mom cooking Thanksgiving dinner.

At about noon, Jimmy came to fetch her and convinced her to come down for lunch.

"We're going to play board games!" He said enticingly through the door. He knew this would get her, she had a naturally competitive spirit.

The dining room table was set up with a Monopoly board, the same one they'd been playing with for decades. When she entered the room, her Dad came to her and gave her a bear hug and a big smooch on the cheek.

"C'mon, Button, you can have the horse," he said as he led her to her seat. Nobody said anything to her about her earlier breakdown. It wasn't because they didn't support her, it was more because they were simply accepting her emotions. That was the nice thing about her family, and Love and Aaron seemed to be taking it all in stride as well.

The chairs were set up the same as they had been since their first breakfast together, with Aaron next to her. So she had Aaron on one side of her and Love on the other, with Jimmy across the table. She had to admit she liked being seated next to Aaron, she could smell his woodsy scent and every time their hands came close to each other when they were moving pieces or counting money, there was a delicious tingle on her skin.

Jenny had the horse, Jimmy had the race care, Rudy took the ship, Aaron chose the dog, and Love chose the wheelbarrow, which Jenny found funny for some reason. She tried to think of a time when anyone in their family had chosen the wheelbarrow and couldn't think of one. She and Jimmy usually argued between the horse and the race car. Rudy usually took the ship or the top hat, sometimes the cannon. Her Mom had always, always, always chosen the thimble. The wheelbarrow had remained untouched for over 20 years in its little compartment inside the Monopoly box. Until today.

Board games were a good way to pass the time on a cold afternoon. They were also a good way to see into someone's personality. Almost two hours later, Rudy was on top of the game, fiercely going after whatever properties he could and putting as many hotels on them as possible. Jimmy and Jenny were scrapping for second place. Love had dropped out of the game fairly early, lacking the hardened emotions necessary to annihilate her opponent. Aaron had lasted longer, but eventually went bankrupt after landing on Park Place and having an especially brutal dealing with its landlord, Rudy.

When it was finally over, Rudy got out pads of paper and pens for everyone, Love piled the cookbooks in the middle of the table, and they set about deciding on what dishes they were all going to focus on. The cookbooks were a combination of her Mom's, which had always lived in this kitchen, and some new ones that Jenny had never seen before, including one called "Eat Your Avocado", that apparently belonged to Aaron.

"Have you made many of these?" Jimmy asked Aaron as he thumbed through the listings of Mango Avocado salad and Avocado pasta sauce.

"Yeah," Aaron looked sheepish. "I'm kind of a food nut."

"Jenny," Love pushed two well used cookbooks towards her, "These must have been a few of your Mom's favorites." She smiled kindly at both Jenny and Jimmy. "Maybe you'll treat us to something you've always loved."

It was becoming increasingly difficult for Jenny to dislike this woman.

"Thank you," was all she said.

"Oh, Jen!" Jimmy had already flipped one of the cookbooks open. "Remember Angel Food Cakes?!" He laughed and turned it around so everyone else could see the picture. "Remember she made one every year and it never looked like this picture?"

Rudy smiled and nodded, a poignant sparkle in his eyes. Jenny laughed, too. She could picture exactly what Jimmy was describing. How they had teased her every year, and they'd all laughed, their Mom laughing the hardest. Jenny made a mental note to include the Angel Food disaster stories in her journal.

"Well, I have no choice but to put Angel Food Cake down as one of mine," Jimmy said, a quiver of emotion betraying his jovial expression.

"That's a great choice, son," Rudy told him.

"And pies! I love making the pies." Jimmy completed his recipe choices by shutting the cookbook in front of him.

"I'm thinking about yeast rolls," Jenny said, actually

looking forward to making them from scratch. "And maybe the green bean casserole?"

"Oh," Love responded, "That sounds delicious. I'll do the sweet potatoes, and how does brussel sprouts and goat cheese salad sound?"

Jenny screwed up her face at the suggestion. You couldn't have that on Thanksgiving, could you?

"That might be nice with Avocado pie," Aaron piped up from the seat next to her. Jenny's scowl increased as she looked at him.

"Avocado pie? On Thanksgiving?" She asked.

"Yes," Aaron stumbled a little bit on his response. "We've had it a few times, everyone always liked it." He hesitated while writing it on the list, looking around at the others for confirmation that it was okay to do so.

Rudy cleared his throat so loud it caught Jenny's attention and she turned her scowl on him. He gave her a meaningful look before speaking, "Jenny, let's be sure to consider some new traditions from other families as well as our own, please."

It wasn't a request, really. Jenny felt heat crawl up her cheeks. She felt like a little girl getting scolded at the dinner table in front of company. They were all looking at her, again.

"Sure," her voice was monotone. She could say the words, but she couldn't fake the emotion. "I'm sure it will be delicious."

She knew, of course, that it wouldn't.

THE COLD DAY finally turned into an even colder night. Jenny had spent the afternoon alternating between having a mediocre time with the new 'family' to sulking in her bedroom. Nothing seemed to cheer her up and even though she knew she was acting like a teenager, she couldn't stop moping about

Thanksgiving dinner. It was silly, really. She couldn't remember ever caring this much about Thanksgiving dinner before now.

Jimmy called to speak with Penny to find out how her day had gone and wasn't able to get through. Paul texted him after a few missed calls to tell him they were heading into the movie theater and would let him know when they were done. This sent Jimmy into his own funk, and her brother's reaction to being in a funk was often to act the exact opposite.

"Who wants to try out the hot tub?" Jimmy asked the room as they were cleaning dinner dishes. He held up two bottles of wine, one in each hand.

"Sounds good," Aaron answered.

"Jenny?" Jimmy pointed at her with one of the bottles. "I think you need a little mellowing out, don't you?"

"Sure." Jenny glanced at the piles of dirty dishes still stacked on the counter next to the kitchen sink.

"Don't you worry about this," Love said to her, "Your Dad and I will take care of it. You kids go have some fun."

And so Jenny was off to her room, searching through drawers for a swimsuit that she may have left behind and that still fit. She finally found one in a plastic tub full of shorts, tank tops and flip flops on the shelf in her small closet. The swimsuit was a tankini, bright aqua with a giant bow positioned right in the middle under her bust. She hadn't worn this suit for over ten years and she barely fit in it, luckily it was a forgiving cut and even though the bow was a little juvenile looking, she wasn't completely disappointed when she checked her reflection in the mirror. The aqua didn't wash her out and was a nice contrast to her nearly auburn hair. Though the fit was tight, it worked to push her not so large bust up, making it appear a little bigger, and when she checked out her backside in the mirror, it looked pretty good.

Lots of walking and trips to the gym helped her out in that arena.

"I'll be in the hot tub most of the time anyway," she said to her reflection, then grabbed a towel and headed downstairs.

Jimmy was already in the hot tub with a half drank glass of red wine in his hand. Steam lifted off the surface of the bubbling water and a green light from somewhere near the bottom illuminated his legs and swim trunks. The night air was bitter cold and though the hot tub was only steps away from the house, the trip in her tankini seemed long. Jenny hurried across the patio and climbed carefully up the steps, her exposed skin shivering.

"Wine?" Jimmy asked, pouring into a second glass before she had a chance to answer.

"Yes, please." Jenny slid into the deliciously warm water and floated down until she found a comfortable indentation on the bench to sit. She took the glass of wine Jimmy offered and leaned into the jet stream that pulsed against her back.

"Cheers?" Jimmy raised his glass and she clinked hers against it.

"Cheers," she answered, taking a sip and turning her head at the sound of the French doors opening. The wine glass never reached her lips, because the instant Aaron walked out of the house wearing only his swim trunks Jenny froze in place.

His hair was down, flowing in wavy glory over his shoulders, a few stray strands tickling at his collar bones. His chest and shoulders were wide, with lean, athletic muscles that flexed slightly as he moved. His abs were strong, with the vague outline of a six pack and a small line of blonde-red hair dropping from his belly button and disappearing under the front of his black swim trunks.

Jenny sucked in her breath as he approached the hot tub.

The litheness of his body reminded her of a thoroughbred racehorse being led to the gates. Jimmy, too, was distracted by Aaron and he let out a very low whistle that only she could hear over the frenzied sound of bubbles.

"It is cold!" Aaron said as he climbed the stairs and lowered himself into the water, his arms and chest rippling slightly with the effort. Jenny realized she was staring and took a quick gulp of her wine.

"It's pretty warm in here," Jimmy quipped, giving her a sideways glance full of amusement. Jenny did her best to ignore him and took another mouthful of wine. What she couldn't ignore was the closeness of Aaron's bare body to her own, the way the water splashed against his chest, how his strong hand carefully held his wine glass, how the tips of his hair got wet and stuck against his shoulders and biceps as if all they wanted to do was touch his skin. That's all she wanted to do. She wanted to reach out and trace her finger up his arm, put her hand under his lush hair and push it back over his shoulder. She wanted to run her fingers through his hair then brush them across his lips and over his beard to see if it was rough or soft. She looked down and realized her wine glass was empty. She was feeling quite warm and tingly.

Aaron and Jimmy were talking, but she had lost track of the conversation. Something about Paul and the struggles of relationships. Aaron was admitting that he'd never been married, never found the right girl. Jimmy was confessing that he couldn't imagine living without Paul for the rest of his life, that he'd thought his marriage was going to last forever.

"Maybe you can work things out," Aaron offered. He grabbed the second bottle of wine and gave Jenny a questioning look, did she want more? She nodded, enjoying the pleasant tingling she was feeling. Aaron moved closer to her, their legs sliding next to each other secretly under the water. He looked at her mischievously as he poured the wine and let his ankle wrap around hers, sending mini shock waves through her body. She didn't look away. "When you find someone you really connect to, you've got to give it your best shot," Aaron said, not taking his eyes off of hers. Those icy blue eyes cut through something inside of her and a shiver started in her belly and moved through her whole body. "Are you cold?" He asked, so close to her, speaking low, his brow furrowed in concern.

"No," she managed to shake her head. "I'm not cold." Her voice was almost a whisper. She felt him move his body closer to hers under the water so their sides were still touching even as he put the wine bottle down. They stayed that way, pressed next to each other in secret, Jenny trying to act as if her heart wasn't leaping out of her chest.

They had polished off both bottles of wine and hashed out Jimmy and Paul's relationship problems when Aaron excused himself to go to bed. Jenny knew she needed to go to bed soon, too. Something in her was afraid to leave at the same time he did, afraid of what might happen once inside the dark house. She and Jimmy watched as Aaron put his hands on the edges of the hot tub and lifted himself out, his glistening wet skin and flexing muscles were almost more than she could handle. He thanked them both and said good night, smiling at her before hurrying back into the heated house. Jenny stared after him, her senses still overwhelmed at the sight and touch of him. Jimmy, who had drank more wine than the other two, propped his arms up on either side of the hot tub. His head dropped back and he closed his eyes, letting out a great sigh.

Then, without looking at Jenny, he spoke up, "Definitely not a little old lady."

Jenny smiled and chuckled at her brother's astute observation. "No, definitely not."

## 7

The next morning in the clearing, Jenny knew exactly what to write about. As soon as the coldest air had given in to the sun's rays and she could write without making her fingers numb, she put down everything she could remember about being in the hot tub with Aaron. The physical sensations, the way the wine softened her, the fluttery way she had felt, was still feeling. Geese flew high overhead, their sounds of their honking were gentle and soothing from so far away. Jenny filled five pages without having to pause and think once. The flow of writing description and emotion took over her senses. So involved in her task, she lost track of how long she had been sitting there and she didn't hear any footsteps until he was practically upon her.

"Jenny?"

She jumped, startled by the noise and Aaron's sudden presence.

"I'm sorry," he said. "I didn't mean to scare you." He was not dressed in running clothes today, but his normal jeans, boots and a dark grey flannel jacket with a blue and green scarf wrapped around his neck. He held the large red plaid thermos in one hand and two thermal mugs in the other. He lifted them up, his eyes dancing. "I brought you something."

Jenny quickly, and hopefully nonchalantly, flipped the green journal closed and smiled at him. "What is it?"

"Hot chocolate, of course. May I?"

Jenny nodded and he sat down next to her, their legs touching, as if the closeness of the hot tub the night before made it normal for their bodies to touch. Somehow, though, it did feel normal and Jenny didn't move or put any distance between them.

"That sounds delicious," she said, placing her journal and pen on the empty bench on her other side. "Thank you."

Aaron carefully unscrewed the lid and poured the steaming hot beverage into one of the cups, which she took gratefully.

"This smells amazing," she told him.

"I made it from an old family recipe," he answered.

"You did?" Jenny looked down at the frothy, chocolaty goodness, impressed.

"How is your writing going?" He asked as he poured a cup for himself.

Jenny shrugged nonchalantly, trying not to look guilty about writing her intimate feelings about him. "Oh, it's fine. I'm really out of practice."

"Don't you write for work?"

"Yes, but this is different." She hesitated for a moment. He waited patiently, watching her over his cup as he blew on the hot chocolate to cool it down. "I've decided to try writing fiction," she added.

Aaron lifted his eyebrows and nodded as he took a sip. "Sounds fun."

"Yeah," she smiled at him, her nerves on high alert, not only because he was so physically close to her, but also because she wasn't sure about sharing her writing plans with anyone.

"What made you decide to do that?" He asked.

Jenny wasn't sure what came over her, perhaps it was the beautiful surroundings of the clearing, or the butterflies in her stomach, or maybe it was the way he leaned back so comfortably next to her, watching and listening with such interest. Whatever the reason, she told him the whole story. She told him about finding the stack of journals with the card from her Mom and then reading through the stories she'd written when she was young. She told him how much she missed creative writing and how she had chosen something more practical for her career.

Aaron listened attentively, his eyes fixed on her, looking into her as she spoke and pulling more and more of the truth out of her. When she stopped talking there was a pause when neither of them said anything. Then Aaron's face broke into a huge smile and he nudged her gently with his shoulder.

"Good for you!"

She blushed and smiled at her hot chocolate. "Thank you."

"That's really cool," he continued. "Have you already started a story?"

She blushed harder, thinking about what she'd just written about him in her journal. "Not exactly. I've just started with some writing exercises."

"Well I think it's great you want to go after something like that, you know? Following a dream."

Something in his tone made her wonder. "Do you have any dreams you wish you would have gone after?"

He thought about it for a moment then nodded. "I do."

Jenny nudged him with her shoulder. "Yeah? What are they?"

He laughed and shook his head 'no'. "Nothing important."

"Come on," she said. "I told you mine."

Aaron looked out across the clearing and thought for a second, then he cocked his head at her and gave her a grin. "I always wanted to be a chef."

"Really?" She was surprised and not surprised. "A French chef?"

"No teasing," he warned with a comical shake of his finger.

She laughed, "I'm not teasing. A chef, huh?" She looked him up and down. "I can see it."

"You can?"

"Sure, you obviously like to cook." She held up her cup as evidence then took a sip. "And this is so good!"

He laughed, "You're definitely teasing me now."

"No I'm not," she smiled. "Love said you worked in finance?" He nodded in response and she continued, "How did you get there from wanting to be a chef?"

"Well, I've always been good with numbers, so that's what my parents, mostly my Dad, wanted me to study. I'm finance director for a natural foods company. So it has all of the stability that my parents drilled into my head and a little something to do with good food."

She understood the connection, but still found it a little sad that he had ended up so far away from what he loved. They sat together quietly, sipping their hot chocolate and looking out over the clearing.

"I guess you'll get a chance to cook up a storm tomorrow," Jenny told him.

"I will." He grinned again. "Oh, by the way, Love said we are all going food shopping together as soon as you and I get back."

DECIDING who would drive into town turned out, to Jenny's embarrassment, to be a thinly veiled attempt at matchmaking. Since Aaron didn't know the way, they all agreed he would be a passenger. Since not everyone could fit into just one car, it was agreed they needed two drivers. Jenny assumed Jimmy would come with her, and Love and Aaron would go in her Dad's car. To her surprise, that is not what happened.

"Son, why don't you ride with us?" Rudy suggested after receiving a barely concealed whisper of instruction by Love.

Jimmy, who had already started towards Jenny's car, paused mid-step.

"Yes," Love chimed in. "And Aaron, why don't you ride with Jenny?" She tried to give it a light hearted spin, like it was just a meaningless idea that had popped into her head with no forethought.

Jenny didn't buy it.

Love nudged Rudy and he spoke up again, "That'll work. Give us a chance to catch up with you, Jim Boy." He reached out his arm towards Jimmy and motioned for him to come over to his car. Jimmy and Aaron exchanged a look. Jimmy shrugged and turned to Jenny, wiggling his eyebrows up and down at her and sideways glancing towards Aaron.

"I'll go with Dad and Love," Jimmy announced.

And that was that. Jimmy climbed into their car leaving Aaron standing on the passenger side of hers.

"Do you mind?" Aaron asked.

"No," Jenny said politely, though she was mortified at the blatant attempt to get her and Aaron alone in a car. "Not at all."

Aaron was much taller than Jimmy and had to adjust the seat all the way back to fit comfortably. It had been a few years since Jenny had had a man in her car and being so close to him she could smell his fresh soapy, leathery scent. She fumbled with her keys a little as he clicked on his seatbelt.

"That wasn't too subtle was it?" Aaron asked.

Jenny laughed, "So it's not my imagination?"

Aaron shook his head in an exaggerated 'no'. "I definitely think they're playing matchmaker."

Rudy, Love and Jimmy pulled past them, Rudy honking and waving at her to follow, as if she didn't know her way to town. Love leaned over and smiled excitedly at them. They could see Jimmy from the back seat giving them a grin and, Jenny thought, a rather sarcastic thumbs up.

"Oh my God, this is so embarrassing," Jenny groaned.

"I think they mean well," Aaron chuckled, then leaned in towards her as if he was going to tell her a secret. "I don't mind if you don't."

Her heart picked up a pace. He was very close, their shoulders touching. She waved her hand as if the whole thing was nothing, meant nothing.

"I don't mind, it's harmless I suppose," she answered.

Aaron settled back into his seat and smiled to himself as she finally found the right key and started the car.

The scenery on the ride to town was magnificent. A lot of the time both Jenny and Aaron were silent as they drove through the brilliant fall foliage. They did manage to spark one significant conversation about Aaron's family when Jenny asked him how long his parents were staying in France.

"Who knows," he answered, a twinge of bitterness in his tone.

Jenny glanced at him. "Do they travel a lot?"

He nodded. "Yes, my parents have never been the type to stay still or even nearby for very long." He didn't look at her as he spoke, but focused on the scenery outside the passenger window. "We never had holidays like this, playing games together, cooking together. They're not the warm, fuzzy types."

"Is that why you spent time at Love's when you were a kid?"

He nodded, "Yep. She's a sweet woman. And her husband was a good man. It was really sad when he passed away."

Jenny understood and felt a pang of guilt over her resentment of Love. She hadn't thought much about Love's past and whether or not she'd suffered loss and pain.

"It's too bad she never had children of her own," Aaron continued, still watching out his window. "She would have been a great Mom."

Apparently everyone in the surrounding area was shopping today. When they reached the town it took much longer than normal to drive through because people filled the sidewalks and flowed in front of their car at the crosswalks. The parking lot of the only grocery store was packed full as was all of the parking on Main Street. Jenny drove around in an ever widening circle until she finally found a space on a side residential street about ten blocks from the grocery store.

Just as she put the car in park, her phone buzzed. It was Jimmy.

"Hey," Jenny answered.

"Where are you?" He asked, "We had to park five miles away because of the crowds!"

"Us too," Jenny informed him as they climbed out of her car. "I guess we'll just meet you at the grocery store?"

"Sounds good," Jimmy agreed before ending the call.

"We're going to meet them there," Jenny informed Aaron, who had joined her on her side of the car.

"Great," he flashed her a smile as he swooped his arm gallantly towards the bustle of Main Street. "Shall we?"

She blushed a little at his invitation and his Nordic blue eyes twinkled.

The day was brisk and cold, but still sunny, a beautiful fall day. Aaron fell into step next to her and Jenny enjoyed how normal it felt, how comfortable, to have him stroll with her down Main Street. He was very much a gentleman, always putting himself between her and the street and even moving in close and lightly touching her back to guide her through large crowds. His height and strikingly attractive Viking look drew stares from more than one woman. Jenny felt a hot spike of jealousy whenever it happened, but noticed that he didn't pay attention to any of them, just continued chatting and laughing with her as they walked. They came across a small, gourmet cooking shop and Jenny saw Aaron's eyes light up.

"Would you like to look around in here?" She asked.

"I'd love to," Aaron said. "Do we have time?"

"Of course." She was happy at the idea of taking a little diversion with him and they popped into the store.

A heavy scent of spices and rich coffee filled the little shop. Though it was small, the room was stuffed from top to bottom with shining pots and pans, ceramic cookware and dishes in bright colors, crisp tea towels, napkins, aprons and oven mitts in vivid patterns, and small, intricate gadgets stored in earthy crocks on tables that groaned under the weight of the merchandise. Jenny and Aaron both paused after entering, enjoying the warmth on their cheeks and the enchanting displays.

"Would you like some mulled wine?" A round faced elderly woman asked them from behind an old fashioned looking cash register.

Aaron looked at Jenny before answering. She gave him a 'why not' face and he stepped towards the cashier, pulling his wallet out of his back pocket.

"Oh, no charge, dear," the lady said, her round cheeks squishing into a smile.

"Thank you," Aaron said. As he waited for the cashier to fill two paper cups with mulled wine out of a silver coffee dispenser, his eyes wandered happily over the items for sale on the counter. He picked up a fat ceramic cup shaped like a chick with a hole in its beak and showed it to Jenny.

"What is that?" She asked, giggling.

"It's to separate egg whites," he explained. "You crack the egg in the top and pour the whites out of its mouth."

"Those are one of my best sellers," the cashier told him as she handed him the mulled wine. Aaron took the cups and handed one to Jenny.

"Thank you," she said, smiling.

The cashier took a second look at her and smiled in recognition. "Oh, hello, aren't you the Combes girl?"

"Yes," Jenny smiled back.

"Aren't you grown up and beautiful, just like your Mom," the cashier continued. Jenny's face stiffened, though she was able to hold onto her smile for the elderly lady's sake. "I remember when your Mom would bring you and your brother in here when you were just little bitty things," the cashier reminisced. Caught up in her own thoughts, she didn't notice how Jenny's good mood had slipped away or how her gaze had dropped so that she stared hard at the red mulled wine in her cup. Aaron looked quickly at Jenny then back at the cashier.

"Do you own this shop?" He asked.

"Yes," the cashier answered proudly.

"How long have you been here?" Aaron asked, stepping a little forward so his body partially blocked Jenny from the cashier's view.

He was trying to shield her, she realized, and was suddenly grateful.

She turned halfway away as if she was looking at a pile of nearby tea towels while Aaron distracted the cashier with small talk. Her stomach roiled slightly and she knew there was no way she was going to be able to finish her drink. The fun excursion with Aaron had turned sour, the warmth of the little store now seemed overwhelming and all she could think about was getting away.

Thankfully, Aaron kept up his distracting conversation long enough to gulp down his drink. When the cashier was busy with another customer, he discreetly took Jenny's still full cup and disposed of it at a trash can near the front then steered her out the front door.

Out in the cool air again, Jenny took a deep breath.

"Are you okay?" Aaron asked, his brow furrowed with concern.

"Yeah," Jenny said, although she wasn't sure it was true. "I'm sorry, it's silly, I just kind of froze," she tried to explain.

"It's not silly and don't be sorry," he told her.

She sighed. She had a real talent for ruining the mood.

"I suppose we should get to the store," she said.

"Lead the way," he answered.

Even though he was being as upbeat as ever, for Jenny, the spell of their walk had been irreparably broken.

## 8

Wednesday morning was warm for the season and the day promised to get even warmer. There was colder weather moving in later in the evening and the next day, Thanksgiving, was supposed to be very cold so Jenny was determined to take advantage of this beautiful weather while it lasted. She headed to the clearing earlier than normal and didn't even have to wear a hat or warm up the tip of her ball point pen by putting it in her mouth before she wrote. She sat down in the bench with the sunrise view and waited for it to be light enough to write. She had a list of stories about her Mom that she wanted to write about today, Thanksgiving stories, holiday stories.

The problem was thoughts of Aaron kept popping into her mind and not going away. The way his eyes twinkled when he flipped crepes, how they'd shared a cart while shopping for food, how he looked when he laughed in the car, how he'd chatted up the overly friendly cashier to try to save her from being sad, the feel of his skin next to hers in the bubbling warm water of the hot tub. Aaron consumed her thoughts and try as she might, she couldn't focus her writing on childhood holiday memories. Her mind had other ideas.

Frustrated, Jenny shoved her pen into the center of the green journal and forced it closed before pushing it all awkwardly back into her jacket pocket. She refused to write about Aaron. That wasn't what this holiday was about. Her sole focus during her time here at the Lake House was supposed to be about her Mom and keeping her memory alive, not having the hots for some guy Love invited here. Besides, Jenny knew that Love wanted her and Aaron to hit it off, and she was having none of it.

Feeling restless and not in the mood to write, she thought maybe she could clear her mind with a walk. She made her way back to the house from the clearing and to the end of the drive, turning at the mailbox onto the path that led all the way to the covered bridge. Going to the bridge might give her new inspiration.

She walked briskly, working off some of her irritation as she moved through the woods. Along the way she saw a few fat squirrels hurrying from tree to tree, one of them chattered angrily at her from the branches. There was a rabbit hiding just underneath the deep rusty red leaves of a chokeberry bush, sitting as still as possible in the hopes that she wouldn't notice him. She kept a wide birth around him, not wanting to scare him out of his hiding place.

By the time she was almost to the covered bridge she had once again found the delight she always enjoyed in these woods. Surrounded by the stunning colors of fall, the magical way the rays of sun shone through the tree canopy, the narrow path carpeted with fallen leaves and the woodland creatures all around, Jenny had always felt a little like a fairy tale character in this place. Even though she was no longer a little girl or a whimsical teenager, a piece of her still believed that wonderful things were possible in this fanciful forest.

The rhythmic sound of footsteps coming from behind her were at once familiar and surprising. She knew before she turned around who it was, and her face brightened with an expectant smile. Aaron, on the other hand, didn't expect to see her standing in the middle of the path where he was jogging.

"Woah!" He exclaimed as he stopped short, breathing hard from the exertion of his run.

"Hi," she gave him a little wave.

"Jenny," Aaron said, letting out a startled laugh as he spoke. "You're here." He tried to catch his breath as he let his eyes slip over her from head to toe, "Not writing today?"

"I thought I'd take a little walk," she answered.

"I see that," he said.

Aaron approached her and stood close, very close. His breath was still rapid, but Jenny was suddenly not sure if it was only because he'd been jogging. He was so near she could breathe in his scent. He looked down into her face, his eyes capturing hers like a magnet. Her heart melted in his gaze. He reached up towards her ear and a thrill filled her body. She leaned towards him, expecting his fingertips to brush her temple then push into her hair and draw her into a kiss. She closed her eyes and held her breath, waiting to feel his lips on hers, the tickle of his beard on her skin. Instead, she felt a tickle on her scalp and opened her eyes. Aaron was still there smiling at her holding up a small, orange oak leaf he had plucked from her hair.

"You're becoming one with the forest," he said, his amusement at her misunderstanding obvious.

Jenny blushed furiously. He must think she was a pathetic, lovesick soul. He probably thought she purposely came down this path to see him on his run. Had she? The thought made her flustered. She'd been so caught up in thinking about him it never crossed her mind that he might not be interested in her. Had she misread everything? Of course she had, that much was clear. It was entirely possible that Aaron had only been being polite towards her the last few days, nothing more.

"Thanks," Jenny smoothed her hair self-consciously. She turned back towards the covered bridge to try to hide her embarrassment. "I just thought, you know, I thought I'd take a walk, go down to the bridge. It's so nice today, nice day for a walk..." Why couldn't she stop talking? She took a few steps to prove that she was, indeed, going to the covered bridge.

"Mind if I come along?" He asked, falling in step next to her.

She shrugged so hard nobody for miles around could have misinterpreted the fact that she didn't care one bit if Aaron joined her on her walk. She pursed her lips together so she wouldn't keep rambling on and on about nothing as they walked. She decided to concentrate mainly on not allowing their arms or hands to brush up against each other.

They made their way silently around the last turn in the path and down a small incline that led to the edge of the river and the covered bridge. There was a dead tree laying over the last section of path, blocking any normal passing. Aaron stepped on top of the most horizontal section of the trunk and balanced, then offered his hand to her.

"Let me help you," he said.

Jenny hesitated, her humiliation of the non-existent kiss still fresh. Aaron beckoned her up with a quick motion of his hand.

"We don't have to go all the way there," Jenny said.

"Come on," Aaron coaxed. "It's clear on this side."

She gave in and reached her hand towards his. He took it in a firm grip and pulled her up on the log in one quick swoop so she was facing him and they were standing just inches away from each other. The log wiggled from their movement and

Aaron held her hand even more tightly, bracing her from falling by putting his other hand on her waist.

"Oh!" Jenny was off center from the moving log under her feet as well as the feeling of being in Aaron's arms, even innocently.

"I've got you," Aaron said, his voice was low and calming. Still, the butterflies in her stomach would not stop fluttering. He held her there for a long moment, warming her with his touch, looking down into her face with an expression Jenny couldn't quite read. Try as she might, she couldn't keep her heart from beating wildly at the closeness of him. Then, without a word, Aaron guided her with his hands and helped her off the other side of the tree, hopping down next to her as soon as she was safely placed on the path.

"Thank you," Jenny said quietly.

"My pleasure."

The old covered bridge was as enchanting as ever. The rays of the morning sun shone through the spaces between the planks, creating an elaborate light and dark pattern inside. Jenny walked in the entrance, wanting to look at the river and trees through the slatted sides. Aaron followed her and something about being together in the quiet shadowed protection of the bridge felt intimate, almost sensual. When he spoke, it was in the same low tone he'd used when he held her close on the log.

"Beautiful," he said. He was standing close at her side as she peered out through the planks at the river, but when she glanced at him he was looking at her, not the river.

"I used to think this bridge was magic," she confessed, not sure why she was telling him. Something about Aaron made her say things she would normally keep inside. She looked back at the river, embarrassed at her secret.

"Magic?" He asked, looking around at the dust particles

dancing in the rays of light. "I can see that. Did you ever have a wish come true here?"

She shook her head 'no. She never had.

They looked at each other for a long moment. His eyes were even more intense in the slatted shadow and light of the bridge. Aaron started to say something to her when the sound of a car coming down the road interrupted them and they stepped out of the covered bridge and off the road. When the car passed and they were safely out of the way Aaron turned to speak, but Jenny was already walking up the path back towards the Lake House.

LATER, when they were gathered back in the house, Love asked Jenny to help her pick out the china to use the next day for Thanksgiving.

They stood together with the doors to the china cabinet open so the different patterns were easier to view. Jenny was struck again at how small and light Love seemed. The older woman was very tiny, not frail really, just a small, thin woman.

"What pattern do you think we should use?" Love asked. Her grey hair was down, long and wavy with little stray pieces floating out of place. Even her hair was lighter than air. She wore jeans and an untucked long sleeve rose colored blouse with pearl buttons. She didn't have on any jewelry except for her wedding ring, a plain platinum band. She also wore no makeup. Jenny had not seen her wear one drop of makeup since they arrived.

"I like these two." Jenny motioned towards the off white pattern with red and gold ribbons on the edges and the hunting pattern, which featured different wild game birds on each size plate as well as a tumbling black and brown leaf patter on the edges.

Love picked up a salad plate with a pheasant on the front, running her finger along the pattern. She flashed an approving smile. "I was hoping you would say this one. I think it's beautiful."

Jenny nodded, her Mom had excellent taste in china, as well as in decor and clothes and everything else.

"We could mix them," Jenny suggested, taking out a larger dinner plate from the plainer pattern and adding another pheasant salad plate to the top.

"Oh, what a wonderful idea!" Love was delighted, she touched Jenny's arm in her excitement. To her surprise, Jenny didn't have to fight the urge to pull away. It felt nice to be part of these decisions and she knew Love was making a concerted effort to include her. She couldn't fault the woman for being kind.

"Hey, are we going to use the little turkeys?" Jimmy joined them. He picked up the small sterling silver individual salt and pepper shakers shaped like wild turkeys that lived inside the china cabinet with all of the finer table dressings.

"Of course!" Love answered, pleased with his interest.

"Shouldn't you be making your pies?" Jenny teased her brother.

"Aaron's gonna help me, we're doing a baking marathon," Jimmy said over his shoulder as he carried five pairs of the tiny turkeys to the table.

"Shall we get everything out and wash it?" Jenny asked. Love nodded in approval.

Soon they were standing at the sink full of hot soapy water, carefully washing, rinsing and drying the china by hand. Jimmy and Aaron had begun their pie marathon, which resembled more of a pie assembly line on the large dining room table as Aaron mixed pastry dough and rolled out pie crust after pie crust and Jimmy carefully shaped each crust into its pie pan then filled them and popped them into one of the double ovens. They made pumpkin, pecan, apple strudel and, last but not least, Aaron's avocado pie, which turned out to look more like key lime. He held it proudly up for Jenny to see it.

"It doesn't look that bad, does it?" He asked.

"It looks great," Jenny quipped. "I just don't know if I want to taste it." She made a face as if a bad flavor was already in her mouth.

"Just wait and see," he said happily, placing the pie in the refrigerator to chill overnight.

"Who's up for ping pong?" Rudy appeared at the top of the basement stairs looking for some opponents to challenge.

"I'm game," Aaron said. He looked at Jimmy, "We're done here, right?"

"Yep," Jimmy said. "Let's do it."

"You coming, Button?" Rudy called to Jenny.

"Yes, we're almost done. I'll be down in a minute," she answered.

When the men had all disappeared downstairs Jenny and Love could hear the distinctive sound of a ping pong ball bouncing back and forth combined with the guy's hooting and hollering.

Jenny shook her head and chuckled, "Boys."

"Yes," Love agreed. She sloshed the dishwater looking for the last few items in the bottom of the sink as she asked, "How do you like Aaron?"

Jenny was a little taken aback. "Aaron?" She thought about him holding her tightly while they stood on the log, then remembered when she'd closed her eyes thinking he was going to kiss her, and her cheeks flushed. "Oh, he seems like a nice guy." Best to be as nonchalant as possible.

"He is, he is a very nice guy."

They were quiet for a few more moments, Jenny focused on not dropping the Thanksgiving china. She hadn't been truly alone with Love since they'd met and it was making her uncomfortable. The air between them seemed to be heavy with an unknown thought, a conversation that wanted to be had. Finally, Love spoke it out loud.

"So, I have a confession to make," she began. Jenny cringed at the statement, not knowing or wanting to know what Love could possibly be ready to confess. She looked at the plate she was drying carefully, avoiding eye contact with her father's wife. Instead of answering Jenny just made a light grunting noise, hoping this would put Love off. It didn't.

"I have known Aaron since he was a tiny little thing, barely potty trained..."

Probably too much information, Jenny thought.

"He was always a really wonderful little boy and now he's a truly wonderful man," Love continued.

"Mmhmm," Jenny agreed, hoping that would end whatever this was. It didn't.

"Of course, I've never met you before this week, but your father has told me so much about you," Love gushed and Jenny was a little terrified of what she was about to say. "Well, because of everything your father told me about you, which he was right I can tell after meeting you," Love tried to butter her up, "I convinced Aaron to come to Thanksgiving so that you two would meet." Love looked at her with eyes wide, like she couldn't believe she'd just admitted to doing this deed. "Is that horrible of me?"

Horrible? That was a strong word, Jenny thought. Presumptuous, meddling, pushy, these were all better descriptors in her opinion. She considered which of these words she should use to correct Love's statement, but then realized she wasn't surprised at her stepmother's confession and, even more shocking, she wasn't upset about it either. Taking her silence as disapproval, Love started talking again.

"I know it was horrible and pushy. And I wasn't being

calculated about it or anything," she tried to explain. "I wanted him to spend Thanksgiving here with us regardless, I just thought it was beneficial that you are both currently unattached and maybe it would all work out into a really romantic love story."

Love stopped talking and smiled hopefully at her. Jenny, despite herself, smiled back.

"Are you upset?" Love asked.

"Not upset, exactly..." She didn't know what else to say. The thought that she and Aaron might be well matched was not an abhorrent idea to her. The fact that Love thought so too was actually a little encouraging. Then another possibility entered her mind and her stomach sank. She looked at Love with growing dismay, hoping against hope that what she was thinking wasn't true. "Love..." she started.

"Yes?" Love answered, open, kind, waiting expectantly for Jenny's next words.

"Does Aaron know you did this?"

## 9

"I still don't understand why you're upset," Jimmy said, his words thinning as he lifted into the air away from her. He was swinging on the tire swing with Jenny pushing him. He'd insisted, citing many moments in their shared childhood when he'd pushed her even when he was suffering from heartbreak or romantic anxiety.

"I don't like people meddling in my life," she answered. Jimmy swung back towards her, twirling a little as he did so she had to step to the side in order to get her hands on his backside to push him again.

"But I thought she said he didn't know she was playing matchmaker," Jimmy asked, his words once again floating high in the air above them.

"Can you keep your voice down?" Jenny requested, worried that Aaron might overhear them.

"Do you think he's gonna pop out of the shrubbery?" Jimmy teased, laughing as he tilted back in the tire swing and pumped his legs. Jenny abandoned her post and sat down cross legged on the picnic blanket they'd brought out and laid at the base of the huge oak tree.

"I don't know where he is," she answered crossly. This was true. Jenny hadn't seen Aaron since the morning. She'd been in the kitchen kneading her yeast rolls when he came to find her, apparently he'd gone looking for her in the clearing.

"Not writing this morning?" He'd asked cheerfully, setting the thermos of hot chocolate down on the counter.

"No, I wanted to get my rolls ready to rise." If he was disappointed she didn't see it, she was laser focused on kneading the ball of dough on the counter top.

She'd pretended that seeing him each morning wasn't any big deal, that she'd forgotten about the last few days, that she had other things to do besides wonder where he was going to be and put herself there. In reality, Jenny had hidden out in her bedroom trying to write, but failing. Instead she'd watched out the window and seen Aaron leave for his run before the sun came up. She then watched him return to the house and leave about 20 minutes later walking towards the clearing, thermos in hand. That's when she'd hurried downstairs to start her rolls, so she would look busy.

"Earth to Jen," Jimmy said. He'd stopped swinging and was hanging almost upside down from the tire waiting for her to answer his question.

"What?" She asked.

"I said," he pulled himself upright and kicked the ground so the tire swing spun slowly, "Do you like him?"

"Aaron?"

"No, Leonardo DiCaprio." Jimmy rolled his eyes in mock frustration. "Aaron, Jen, do you like Aaron?"

Jenny looked at her brother, but didn't say a word. She clamped her lips together to keep from blurting out an answer. Heat rose in her cheeks and she tried to look angry.

"You do!" Jimmy declared, pointing an accusing finger at her as he kicked the tire swing into a faster twirl.

"It doesn't matter," Jenny retorted. "That's not the point!"

"That is exactly the point," Jimmy argued. He scraped his feet in the dirt, stopping the twirling tire so he could look her straight in the eyes. "If you like him and he likes you, what does it matter how you met or who introduced you or even why they did?"

Jenny opened her mouth to answer, but Jimmy was on a roll.

"Jen, you're always doing this. You're always pushing good things away, like you think you don't deserve them or don't want to be happy or something." His eyes teared up as he continued, "It's not every day you come across someone who you could fall in love with, and when you do, you shouldn't throw it all away on a...on a technicality."

Jenny could see that they were no longer talking about her situation alone.

"Is that what I do?" She asked him meekly.

He nodded then sighed. "We both do."

They sat quietly for a while, Jenny hugging her knees at the base of the oak tree and Jimmy dangling from the same tree, scuffing his feet in the dirt.

"Sucks to be us," Jenny said. Jimmy laughed so suddenly he snorted, which made her laugh.

"Think of it this way, at least she didn't try to fix you up with some horrible, ugly, jerk of a guy," Jimmy said. "I mean, he's got a good job, he's nice, he can cook, and he's gorgeous...truly gorgeous!!"

Jenny laughed again and stretched her leg out to push the tire swing away with her foot.

"Help me! Help me!" Jimmy continued, keeping the swing just out of her reach and flailing his arms around as if he was in great peril. "I've been set up with an Adonis!"

"Daddy! Daddy!" A little girl's voice rose above their laughter and they both turned to see Penny running around the house into the back yard.

"Penny?" Jimmy's face went from confusion to sheer joy at the sight of his daughter. He scrambled to climb out of the tire swing and made it just as she reached the tree. She raised her hands towards him and he swept her into his arms.

"Daddy!" She said into his neck.

"Penny, Pumpkin, how...?" The answer to his question came before he could finish forming it as Paul made his way around the house and into the back yard.

Paul was tall and lanky, with dark hair, eyes and a complexion that he always said came from his mish-mashed ancestry that had all melted together when they fell in love and had babies in America.

Jenny's heart leapt with joy at the look on Paul's face. He didn't look like a man on the brink of divorce, he looked like a man long separated from the one he loved and now within sight of that person once again. He walked purposefully towards his husband and daughter. Jenny could see that Jimmy was openly crying as he held Penny tightly to his chest and Paul approached. She stood up, intending to go and leave them some privacy. Paul gave her a quick nod and a teary smile as she did. She beamed back at him, so happy to see him, so happy he had come for Jimmy's sake.

Her Dad and Love stood in the open French doors off the dining room, watching with joy filled expressions. Jenny could see Aaron standing behind them. Paul wrapped his long arms around Jimmy and their daughter and they stood there together for a few minutes, Jenny and the others stayed still, afraid if they moved they would break the spell that surrounded the reunited family. Jenny couldn't make out what Jimmy and Paul were saying to each other, but she could hear the low tones of their voices punctuated with Penny's soprano tones every now and then. Finally, she did hear Paul's voice bellow out from their hug circle.

"It's freezing out here!"

Everyone laughed and the three of them broke slightly away from each other so they could see the rest of their family.

"Hi Aunt Jenny!" Penny exclaimed, giving her a little wave.

"Hi, honey!" Jenny stepped forward and gave Penny a kiss on her round little cheek, then kissed Paul's cheek as well. He gave her shoulders a squeeze. "I'm so glad you're both here!"

"So are we," Paul answered.

"Where's Grandpa?" Jenny craned her neck to see past the adults around her, looking for Rudy.

"Why don't you all come inside where it's warm?" Rudy called from the patio. "We've got breakfast almost ready."

"We?" Paul looked at Jimmy and Jenny curiously.

"Dad cooks now," Jimmy explained with a 'who knew' shoulder shrug. They all started towards the house when Jenny remembered the blanket. She went back to get it, still smiling at the joy she'd seen on Jimmy's face. She picked up the blanket and shook it, but the dry leaves from the ground were holding fast to the fuzzy material and barely any of them came loose.

"Need some help with that?"

Jenny's stomach did a back flip at the sound of his voice. She turned just as Aaron stooped over and picked up the opposite end of the blanket.

"Thanks," she said, trying to remain calm.

They spent a few moments using one hand to hold up the blanket and the other to brush off dried leaves. The sounds of the family reunion inside the kitchen drifted over the back yard and made her smile.

"It's great your brother's family made it," Aaron suggested, smiling at her. The look on his face made her a little weak at the knees.

"Yes, I'm so happy for him."

"I can see," Aaron said. He glanced at the tire swing hanging still nearby. "I also noticed that you didn't get a chance to swing."

"Oh," Jenny shook her head with a laugh. "Jimmy was hogging the swing. Story of my life." Aaron chuckled.

They brushed most of the debris off the blanket. The next step came naturally, almost like a dance that they both knew. Taking a corner in each hand, they stepped away from each other so the blanket was a large rectangle between them, then they folded it once over, and once over again, before walking towards each other joining their folded corners. Their hands touched at that point sending a jolt of electricity through her. Aaron's eyes smiled at the corners and he tilted his head in that way he did when he thought something was funny.

"Hop on." He took her corners from her and completed the folding of the blanket on his own. "I'll push you."

"Oh, no, you don't have to do that."

"I'm not doing it because I have to," he answered as he placed the folded blanket carefully on the grass in the lawn. He stepped to the tire swing and held it as if he was a chauffeur opening the door to a limousine. "C'mon, it'll be fun!"

"It's getting colder every minute. It's supposed to start snowing!"

"All the more reason to do it now. It could be your last chance." He cocked his head at her, eyes twinkling.

Jenny couldn't think of any more reasons why she shouldn't. So she did.

Soon she was sitting in the center of the tire, her hands gripping the rope. Aaron bent behind her, his hands placed on either side of the tire, his chest brushing against her shoulders, his mouth close to her ear.

"High or low?" He asked, his breath tickling her neck.

"High," she answered, "as high as you can go."

"You sure?"

She nodded, a thrill building in her stomach, "I'm sure."

Aaron pulled her backwards so she hung in the air facing almost straight down and she had a moment to consider how high Aaron could actually go. Then he was running forward, moving her in front of him and over him as he lifted her above his head and ran his full height underneath, sending her whooshing in a great swoop towards the branches of the tree.

Jenny squealed with delight as the cold air rushed past her, biting her cheeks and ears as she held tight to the rope. The tire turned as it flew, so one moment she was facing the tree, then the sky, then the ground. She reached the peak of the swing and relished the feeling of floating high in the air with nothing around her for an instant before gravity did its duty and pulled her back towards the ground. She squealed again. As she swung to and fro snow started falling in light flurries.

"It's snowing!" She exclaimed.

"Are you done?" Aaron asked, "Or do you want to go again?"

"Again!" Jenny laughed. Snowflakes tickled her face and hands, wet and cold, as she felt Aaron's powerful body take hold of her, his strength pushing her up and up until she was flying through the air once more.

Soon it was too cold to continue. Her hands were like ice and she wasn't sure if she could hang on to the rope any longer. She swung slower and slower, passing back and forth in front of Aaron until he was able to grab the tire and bring her to a stop in front of him.

"I think my hands are frozen," she laughed.

"Here," Aaron wrapped his hands around hers on the rope. Jenny was surprised that despite the fact that it was snowing, his strong hands were still incredibly warm. He helped her extricate herself from the tire and before she knew what was happening, they were standing just inches from each other with his hands holding hers. Snowflakes had collected on his shoulders and in his hair. The blue of his eyes was even more pronounced against the grey snowy skies than it was normally, or maybe it was because he had been laughing.

Even with the snow falling harder around them, Jenny felt like she was in a bubble of light. He pulled her closer to him, holding her hands to his chest. His eyes held her in place and Jenny couldn't stop looking into them. He was warm and strong and she wanted to lean into him, let him wrap his arms around her and make her warm and safe.

"You look..." Aaron's voice cracked as if his throat was dry. He stopped what he was saying and cleared his throat, never letting go of her hands. "You're beautiful," he said. Jenny felt a piece of her heart melt into his.

Snow swirled around them, silencing anything else, as if they were the only two people in the world.

## 10

Thanksgiving Day was full of fun and preparation. Love invited Penny to help her stuff the turkey and everyone else talked and laughed as they worked on their assigned dishes and helped set the magnificent table. Places were rearranged and extra china prepared to accommodate Paul and Penny's arrival. Instead of Jenny and Jimmy sitting on one side with Aaron on the other, it was now Jimmy, Penny and Paul on one side and Jenny seated next to Aaron on the opposite side. Dad and Love kept their places at the ends of the large dining table.

Having Penny around was a treat for everyone. She was such a smart and fun loving little girl, always interested in helping, which was adorable. Jenny saw how enchanted Love was with her and it warmed her heart towards the newest member of their family. She could not have accepted a woman who didn't like children, even if she was married to her father.

Penny took an interest in Aaron right away. Maybe it was because of his Viking looks, his long hair, his easy manner, or just that Penny, having two Dads, had grown up very comfortable around men. Whatever the reason she warmed up to him quickly when he let her help him get the wood ready in the fireplace. With the snow picking up outside, it was a perfect day to have a fire. Jenny overheard their conversation as they sat on the hearth.

"You have long hair," Penny told Aaron as she handed him a piece of newspaper.

"Yes, so do you," Aaron answered, crumpling up the newspaper to fill the bottom of the fireplace.

"Mine is this long." Penny pulled her dark hair forward so it laid over her chest. "How long is yours?"

"I'm not sure." Aaron reached up and let down his man-bun, shaking his head so his hair fell down in a wavy mass. "Is it as long as yours?" Penny pulled a piece of his hair forward over his shoulder to compare. "Yours is longer, you win!" Aaron said. Penny giggled.

Throughout the day the turkey cooked and they all munched on veggies and dip and delicious slices of salami and cheese that Paul had brought as his contribution to the meal. There was football playing on the basement TV as well as an endless rotation of ping pong games. While upstairs a fire roared and some old R&B played in the sitting room. The whole house was full of the smell of food cooking and the sound of laughter.

And no matter where she went, Jenny found Aaron at her side.

He brought her drinks from the kitchen, sat next to her to watch the fire and visit with Love and her Dad. He challenged her to a ping pong game and offered her and Penny his spot on the sectional sofa to watch football on TV when they carried in the popcorn.

"You girls can have my place," he said, moving to stand up and make room for them.

"No," Jenny smiled at him, ignoring the fact that Jimmy

and Paul were observing from their position on the couch and, no doubt, coming to their own conclusions about her and Aaron's relationship, "We can fit." She sat down very close to Aaron, so close their legs couldn't help but touch and he had to lift his arm over the back of the couch so their shoulders weren't rubbing. She patted the space next to her for Penny to climb up, which snuggled the little girl nicely between Jenny one side and Paul on the other.

Jimmy and Paul gave each other a look. Jenny pretended not to notice. She enjoyed being this close to Aaron. With his arm up behind her it felt like she could nestle into him and let him keep her warm and protected. He smelled so good and as they shared a bowl of popcorn she thought she could get used to this feeling.

Soon it was time to get dressed for Thanksgiving dinner. Jenny had always loved this ritual. Silly as it may seem, it made her feel like a princess or a fine lady who lived in a great house and had servants. Getting dressed for the evening meal made the holiday all the more special.

Up in her room, she brushed out her hair and pulled it up into a loose bun, which it was barely long enough to accomplish, but she got it done and liked the result. She slipped into a wine colored mid-thigh length dress with a halter neckline that fit well and showed off her shoulders. She touched up her makeup adding an extra dab of deep red lipstick for drama then put on a pair of crystal teardrop earrings she saved for special occasions. She had only brought a pair of black ballet slipper shoes, as she hadn't planned on having to look too impressive. Nevertheless, Jenny was pleased when she studied her reflection in the mirror.

As she made her way down the stairs into the front sitting room, Jenny had no doubts that Aaron was pleased as well. From his position on the sitting room couch he could see her descending the stairs and his eyes lit up when she appeared.

He stood up as if he'd been waiting for her, as if they were going on a date. She smiled at him, unable to contain her reaction.

If she was being honest, she was impressed with his clothing choice for the evening. He wore a pair of black slacks, nicely fitted, black leather shoes, a crisp long sleeved white shirt buttoned at the cuffs and unbuttoned at the neck, and a pair of black suspenders. His beard was lustrous and his hair tumbled over his shoulders, loose and blonde and amazing. As she watched him watch her, a delectable shiver went down her spine.

The table looked amazing. All of the china and silver shimmered under the dozen orange, red and deep brown tapered candles set down the center. A huge flower arrangement of sunflowers, red daisies and orange roses that Love had ordered sat in the very middle. As a final touch, Rudy and Love had folded each deep red cloth napkin into the shape of a turkey.

They all oohed and awed over the beautiful table, taking pictures of one another using it as the backdrop and getting one picture of everyone by using Paul's timer on his camera. Then it was time to get everything on the table. In a kind of water bucket brigade fashion, they passed dish after dish after dish to the table until it was packed full. Then everyone but Rudy and Love sat down and waited for their hosts to carry the golden brown turkey to the table for carving.

As they sat waiting, Aaron leaned over to Jenny putting his hand on her knee to get her attention. His eyes glittered in the candlelight and his long hair brushed against her bare shoulder. His hand was warm, almost hot on her skin and her heart fluttered as she tipped her head to hear what he had to say.

"You look fantastic, Jenny."

She smiled coyly at him and turned slightly so her mouth

was close to his ear. "You do too." He squeezed her knee and left his hand resting there, as if that was where it belonged.

"This bird is heavy!" Rudy declared as he carried the turkey to the table. He looked dapper in his blue shirt and grey sport coat and Love shimmered in a charcoal grey lace dress next to him. Before they said grace, Love read a poem from a slim, blue book. The words were lovely, but complicated, and Jenny forgot them almost as soon as Love read them, but she got the gist of the poem. Love conquers all was the basic message.

"Let's say grace," Rudy said and they all held hands and bowed their heads.

Jenny's hand rested comfortably in Aaron's and she thought again how much she enjoyed his touch.

"Lord," Rudy began, "We thank you for this glorious bounty you've given us today and all the blessings you give us every day. We thank you for this beautiful place to gather together, the time you've allowed us all to be here and both the old and the new friends and family that are gathered around this table."

A terrible thought struck her as she listened. Jenny's heart lurched.

"We have all lost loved ones, my dear Suzanne and Love's husband Carl to name a few of our most precious. We have also known the joy of finding spouses and having children and are grateful to you for the millions of ways you take care of us through the love of others."

Overwhelmed with shame, Jenny could no longer bow her head. As her father spoke she looked around at the bowed heads of everyone at the Thanksgiving table and felt the horrible stab of grief over the one who was missing, her mother, Suzanne Combes.

She was a terrible daughter. How could she sit down at this table on this day in her mother's own house with her mother's own china in front of her and not think about her one time? Not once had the memory of her mother crossed her mind since they'd come in to eat, since Aaron had swung her on the tire swing, since yesterday. Had it truly been that long? She couldn't even remember!

Her father continued saying grace, but Jenny was no longer listening. Aaron continued holding her hand, but Jenny's heart was far away from him, from everyone. Her heart was back with her mother. Where it should be. Though the Thanksgiving meal would take place, Jenny would not enjoy it. The guilt of forgetting stewed inside of her and she resolved that she would not forsake her mother's memory again. Not for anything or anyone, especially not for a trifling flirtation with a man she barely knew.

## ❧ 11 ❧

Her pen flew over the pages of her green journal, recounting not only Thanksgiving memories, but memories of other holidays, of Christmas Eves and Easter mornings, of Halloween costumes and fireworks on the Fourth of July. The storm had moved on and the morning sun was brilliant on the day after Thanksgiving, bouncing its rays off of the thin blanket of newly fallen snow. Jenny had bundled up, brought a dark blue wool blanket and the big brush she used to scrape snow off of her car to the clearing so she could clean off the bench and enjoy this gorgeous, crisp morning with her writing.

She was wasting no time describing all of the most precious thoughts she wanted to remember about her Mom. She'd actually started her writing streak after Thanksgiving dinner as soon as she'd been able to get away from the others. Feigning sleepiness, Jenny had excused herself to her room. With the journal in front of her on her desk by the window in the room her Mom had decorated with her, she'd begun putting her thoughts into sentences and forming the sentences into stories. Sometimes funny, often poignant, she stayed up until after midnight writing then rose early to continue.

Maybe it was because of the soft snow covering the ground, or maybe it was because she was so engrossed in crafting a description of the dollhouse she'd gotten for her eighth birthday, either way she didn't hear any footsteps until he was right there beside her.

"Mind if I join you?"

Jenny looked up to see Aaron wearing his favorite grey flannel with his blue and green scarf and an addition of a matching blue and green hat. The knit hat was the long, slouchy style she'd seen snowboarders wear and came complete with a pom-pom that flopped at the back. Despite the interruption and her resolution to focus on writing about her Mom, Jenny smiled. With the hat and his beard and the snow covered surroundings she couldn't help but think of him as some kind of gnome or elf. A tall, strikingly handsome elf.

Jenny reasoned that she couldn't very well send him away, even if he was interrupting her writing. So she motioned towards the wool blanket she'd spread over the bench to help keep her warm. Aaron sat down.

"I brought a special treat." He lifted the familiar plaid printed thermos and two thermal mugs.

"Oh? What is it?"

Aaron twisted off the lid of the thermos and lifted it up to her nose. The enticing smell of rich coffee with Bailey's Irish Creme drifted with the steam out of the top. She raised her eyebrows in surprise.

"I thought it might be nice with the snow," he grinned. "Would you like some?"

"Please."

Aaron handed her a thermal cup and moved close so he could carefully pour the hot liquid into it. "It looks like your writing is going well," he said.

She nodded, taming the butterflies in her stomach at having him so close. "It is."

"What are you working on?" He finished pouring hers and started on his, then added, "If you don't mind sharing."

"I don't mind." She took a sip of her coffee, burning her lip a little. "I'm writing about my Mom, mostly. Memories of her during the holidays and when I was a kid."

"Oh, wow," Aaron said. "That must be challenging. Although I could see you were really into it." A thought came to him and he looked into her eyes, "Would you like me to go? I don't want to interrupt you."

She shook her head 'no' and took another sip. "I don't mind the break. I've been at it since last night anyway, gotten a lot done."

"Have you? Anything you want to share?"

Jenny felt suddenly shy as she laid her hand on the journal she'd put down on the bench. "Oh, you don't want to hear any of this."

"Sure I do," he said. "I would love to hear something you've written."

"Really?"

"Really."

She knew she shouldn't do it. What she was supposed to be doing was forgetting about him. The urge to shrug him off and tell him 'no' was strong, but something in her wanted to share this with him more than it wanted to hide.

"Okay, I'll need a little liquid courage first." She took a big gulp of her Bailey's coffee making Aaron laugh, then placed it on the bench. She flipped through the pages of her journal, being careful not to look at anything towards the front which she knew held page after page of her impressions of him half naked in the hot tub. Fingers trembling, not from the cold, and cheeks growing hot, not from the spiked coffee, Jenny found a suitable passage. It was a short memory about when she was twelve and they'd been snowed in on Christmas Eve during a blizzard. "Here we go," she said, clearing her throat before starting to read.

"Snow, snow and more snow fell to the ground that day. Not fell, exactly, plummeted was more like it. Big, fat, heavy flakes, sometimes bending to the wind that blew mercilessly, but mostly dropping from the sky in great quantity and building a deep, quiet blanket on everything and everyone who happened to be outside."

Jenny looked up, wondering what Aaron thought so far, not sure about continuing if he didn't like it.

"That's good," he said, smiling at her with his twinkly eyes. "Is there more?"

She nodded. "Do you want to hear more?"

"Yes." Aaron raised his cup to her in an encouraging gesture. Jenny continued.

She read to him about her Dad announcing they were not driving anywhere in the blizzard, her Mom insisting they all get dressed up in the church clothes they would have worn to the Christmas Eve candlelight service. She read to him about her Mom getting out all of their extra candles and finding a couple of Christmas Carol music sheets so Jimmy could play them on his keyboard and they could have their own private candlelight service. She read to him about singing Silent Night and lighting their candles and afterwards, how her Dad had put an Elvis Christmas album on and pulled her Mom into the middle of the living room to dance. She read about how fun and magical it was, how perfect.

When she was done she looked at Aaron, who was concentrating on the snow covered ground in front of them as he listened. He lifted his gaze to hers, his icy blue eyes glistening.

"So, what do you think?" She asked.

"That was wonderful, Jenny," he said. A little thrill shimmered through her when he said her name. "It was sad and sweet...and, man...you're really, really good!" She smiled, blushing hard at the compliment as she closed the journal and put it down on the bench. "I just...I don't know what to say," Aaron continued. She giggled a little at his reaction. He seemed overcome. "Can I...can we...actually, I do know what I want to say." He turned towards her with surprising intensity. "I have something I want to say to you and I hope it's not too...I hope I'm not assuming too much."

"Okay," Jenny answered slowly, not sure what to expect.

Aaron dropped his head and looked at his lap, searching for the right words. When he looked up again she was taken aback by his expression, it was happy and hopeful and full of intention.

"I have something to confess. Three times in the past few days I have wanted to kiss you." Jenny's heart jumped into her throat. "Three times I've had to stop myself from doing the thing that seems like the most natural thing in the world when I look at you, to take you in my arms and kiss you." He reached forward and put his hand on hers, its warmth spreading through her hand and into the rest of her body. "I don't know if you feel the same, and I know maybe this is fast." He shook his head as if he couldn't believe what he was saying either. "But I have to tell you that I have never felt this way about anyone before. You're intelligent and funny and amazing and I want to kiss you right now. I want to have a thousand more chances to kiss you."

Jenny was lightheaded, her breathing shallow and fast. Aaron's eyes were locked on hers, looking into her, pleading with her for what he most desired. Her gaze dropped momentarily to his lips and a powerful surge of attraction pulled them closer to each other. She knew his lips would be warm, insistent, powerful, and they were only inches away. She looked up at him through her lashes, feeling his hand wrap completely around hers. She breathed in and smelled the crisp morning air that surrounded them mixed with his warm, Irish Creme breath.

Then she uttered one, simple word, "No."

He stopped. A wall slammed down around her and she blocked the connection that had been pulling them together. She slipped her hand out of his as he loosened his grip, letting her go.

"Okay." He looked crestfallen and confused. "I'm sorry, I thought–"

"Don't be sorry," she tried to explain. "It's just, you know, I'm not sure I'm in a good place." Jenny realized she was about to start talking uncontrollably, her nerves were taking over. "And you live in Colorado, I live in Illinois, that's really far apart. And there's Love, I'm still not sure how I feel about all of that." She waved her hands in front of her, deflecting his offer, puzzled by her own excuses. She stood up quickly, not wanting to explain anymore, not wanting to look into his beautiful eyes again and face what she'd just rejected. "Excuse me," she muttered, and left the clearing as fast as she could without running.

## 12

Great deals at the day after Thanksgiving sales beckoned and Jenny was afraid she would be doomed to drive Aaron in her car again. Luckily, Penny didn't want to go shopping and both of her Dads didn't really want to take a reluctant five-year-old with them, so Jenny volunteered to babysit. She led Penny downstairs to pick out fun movies to watch for the day while the adults got ready to leave. She heard Aaron return from the clearing and fought the urge to eavesdrop from the bottom of the basement staircase.

In the end, Jenny didn't know who drove which car and what people rode along. All she knew was by the time she and Penny emerged from their first round of movie fun downstairs for a snack the house was empty. Relief tinged with sadness flooded over her, but she decided to focus on being the best Aunt Babysitter of all time and not wallow in self-pity.

She and Penny painted their toes and fingernails, played Chutes and Ladders, went for a walk outside to look at the melting snow and made a tiny 'fairy' snowman. Then they ate leftover turkey sandwiches for lunch. Afterwards, they went up to Jenny's room and she let Penny choose some of the books off of her old bookshelf to read before nap. They only made it through one and a half books before they both fell asleep.

Jenny opened her eyes to gentle shaking and found Jimmy and Paul standing over her smiling. She rubbed her eyes and looked around the room, Penny was still fast asleep in a warm little ball next to her on the bed.

"What time is it?" She mumbled.

"Don't worry, Paul already took a picture," Jimmy whispered as he sat gently at the foot of the bed.

"I did," Paul assured her, "but it was very flattering, trust me." Paul grabbed her desk chair and pulled it over to the side of the bed. "Are you awake enough for an interrogation?" He asked quietly.

"An interrogation about what?" She whispered.

"What have you done to that boy?" Paul asked, his face all seriousness, his eyes teasing.

"What?" She was still a tad groggy. She looked at Jimmy, the only other boy in the room.

"Not him," Paul dismissed Jimmy with a wave of his hand. "Aaron...what have you done to Aaron?"

Jenny carefully sat up a little, trying not to disturb her niece.

"I don't know what you're talking about."

"You should have seen him today," Jimmy explained. "Moping around like a lovesick puppy." Jimmy looked at Paul to corroborate his story.

"Oh yes, he's absolutely miserable, like a sad, gorgeous Viking, " Paul agreed. "We figured something was up since you two have been connected at the hip for the last few days, all doe eyes and giggles." Paul poked her ribs playfully.

A flicker of pleasure passed through her at the news

before she could stop it. She didn't want to feel good if Aaron was missing her. That wasn't the mature thing to do.

"I didn't do anything...really," she defended herself, but it was a weak defense and her brother and brother-in-law caught onto it immediately.

"What happened?" Jimmy grabbed her foot and shook it up and down. The bed bounced a little and Penny murmured in her sleep.

"Stop, you're going to wake her up," Jenny chastised him.

"Do tell us what magic you have used on that delicious morsel of a hipster to turn him into such a pathetic pile of emotional mush," Paul said.

"I didn't mean to hurt his feelings," Jenny admitted. "You shouldn't be happy if he is unhappy anyway."

"We're not happy, Jen," Jimmy said. "We're intrigued!"

"It probably doesn't have anything to do with me," she suggested.

"Nope, sorry, that's impossible. Every time anyone brought up your name his handsome little face would fall and he kind of slumped over and did the Charlie Brown sad walk," Jimmy informed her.

"Every time," Paul agreed.

"He did not," she argued, though secretly hoped this was true. No, that wasn't kind. She didn't want Aaron to be sad. She didn't want him to feel as bad as she did.

"What's the bump in the road?" Paul asked, his interest turning more towards concern. "You know, we're old pros at getting past romantic obstacles." He smiled lovingly at Jimmy who winked back at him. "Maybe we can help?"

She flopped her head back on the pillow and let out a groan. "No, there's nothing you can do."

"Why not?" Jimmy wanted to know. "You like him, Jen. We can all see it. Now, what's the problem? Is it that he's too handsome and thoughtful? Do you need someone more aloof with a quirky look?"

"Don't be mean," Jenny said.

"I'm not being mean," Jimmy said.

"He's not trying to be mean," Paul explained. "It's just so frustrating to watch. You two looked so happy together!"

There was a soft knock on the bedroom door and Jenny sat up. They all looked at each other like they'd been caught by their parents cussing in the tree house. She cleared the sleep out of her throat.

"Come in?"

The door clicked and pushed open revealing Aaron standing sheepishly in the hallway, her green journal in his hands. Jenny's mouth went dry.

"Sorry." Aaron took in the three of them huddled together at Jenny's bed, then noticed Penny still sleeping. He spoke quietly, "I wanted to bring this to you. You left it..." His voice trailed off and Jenny swore she saw his cheeks redden under his beard. She scrambled up from the bed, making the mattress bounce and waking up Penny.

"Daddy?" Penny said to Paul and Jimmy both.

"Hi honey, how was your nap?" Paul lifted her up in her still sleepy state and moved to carry her out of the room.

"I hope I didn't wake her," Aaron said, looking genuinely bothered at the idea.

"Oh, no," Jimmy answered as he stepped to Paul's side and they both slipped towards the door. "Come in," Jimmy waved Aaron into the room. "We were just leaving."

There was an awkward bottleneck at the doorway as Paul and Jimmy tried to give Jenny and Aaron some privacy and Jenny and Aaron tried not to look like they were about to have some privacy.

Finally, it was just Aaron remaining in her room. He looked

tall and manly next to her girlhood furniture. Even with his wide shoulders, epic mane of hair, strong cheekbones and piercing blue eyes, there was a terrible vulnerable pain in his face and Jenny couldn't help but feel bad for her part in putting it there.

"So this is your room?" He said, his cheeks definitely red this time.

"Yeah," Jenny was at a loss for words. There had never been a man in this room except for Jimmy, Paul or her Dad.

"Anyway," Aaron dipped his head, looking down at the journal before holding it out to her. "I wanted to get this back to you this morning, but we left right away and you weren't around."

Jenny took it, sensing the nearness of his hand to hers. She wondered if he'd read any more of it, if he'd seen the parts when she wrote about wanting to touch his hair or how the water splashed onto his chest in the hot tub.

"Thanks," was all she managed to say.

"Sure, well–"

"Aaron," she interrupted, clutching the journal to her stomach. "I'm sorry."

He paused, "For what?"

"For this morning, for–"

"Saying no?" This time he interrupted her, holding up his hand to stop her from saying anything else. "Don't be sorry for that, Jenny. I would never want to do anything...I mean, a woman has the right to say what she wants."

Jenny nodded, still clutching the journal. Aaron sighed and looked at the ground, then raised his eyes to hers from under his brow.

"I'm the one who should be sorry. I brought it up and now everything is awkward." He gave her a half smile. She smiled back.

"It's not awkward," she tried to deny.

"You don't find this awkward?" He looked at her disbelieving. "I do!"

She laughed at that, which made him chuckle. He shifted his weight from one foot to the other and seemed to relax as her laughter subsided.

"I guess it is a little awkward," she said.

He nodded, "Yeah, but I think maybe it will wear off." He turned sideways as if he was about to leave, then looked back at her once more, a genuine smile crinkling the corners of his eyes. "You think we can be friends?"

She let the question hang in the air for a moment, believing that once they agreed to it there was no turning back. Her fingers held tight to her journal as she felt herself drawn into his eyes one last time, letting him look into her and hoping that what he saw would help him understand.

"Yes, of course," she said, and as soon as she said it she felt him withdraw from her, respectfully.

When he was gone, Jenny sat down on the side of her bed still holding tight to her green journal, her palms sweaty and her heart beating slow and heavy in her chest. She'd made the right decision, surely she had. What she didn't understand was why making the right decision made her feel like the world had just been ripped out from under her feet.

## 13

On her last morning walk to the clearing, Jenny lingered, taking in the feel of the earth under her boots, still heavy with the weight of melted snow. Many leaves had fallen in the storm and now lay in a thick, squishy layer along the path. Some of fall's colors were still present in the limbs above her, but the snow had been cold enough to turn much of the brilliance to brown and it was only a matter of time before all of the leaves would fall and turn into mulch on the ground.

She was sorry to see the wonder of autumn go. Perhaps it would make leaving tomorrow to return home to her condo and her job more tolerable. Perhaps not. She took in a deep breath and smelled wet woods and damp leaves. The glow of dawn was getting stronger, illuminating the path and the detailed texture of the bark on the trees as she moved towards the clearing.

Settling into her bench to watch the morning break, Jenny tried to think about anything but Aaron. Since their discussion in her bedroom they had managed to be civil and even friendly towards each other at dinner and the game of cards that followed. Jenny didn't accept Jimmy's invitation to join him and Paul in the hot tub, saying she had a headache and was going to bed. She noticed that Aaron didn't join them either and wondered if he'd refused for the same reasons she had.

Today was the last day of Thanksgiving vacation. She was leaving tomorrow morning, a blessing and a curse. On one hand, she wouldn't have to go through any more encounters with Aaron, which was a relief. On the other hand, the knowledge she wouldn't see him again after today left her with a deep sense of longing.

The same problem faced her this morning. She knew that Aaron knew where she was. Would he come to see her? Or not? Both options were wholly unsatisfactory. She took in a deep breath and let out a heavy sigh.

"That's why it's a good thing that everything is over tomorrow," she said out loud, her voice drifting into the calm morning air.

"Talking to yourself?"

Jenny turned quickly in her seat, startled by the voice even though she recognized it immediately.

"Dad?"

Rudy appeared from the woodland path, and walked over, joining her on the bench.

"It's a little cold out here this morning, isn't it?" He lifted his shoulders up and down as if trying to warm his muscles and shoved his hands into his pockets.

"A little," she agreed. "What are you doing out here so early?"

"Oh, I don't mind getting up early every now and then." He looked around the clearing, the sunrise had officially begun and the golden hour of light made everything around them shimmer. "Sure is pretty."

"Yeah," she answered.

They sat together silently for a few minutes enjoying the sunshine as it grew stronger and warmed their faces.

"Your Mom loved watching the sunrise out here, you know," he said. He looked at her with a grin. "You look just like her sitting here."

Tears filled Jenny's eyes and she smiled back at him without answering. Her Dad took one hand out of his jacket pocket and patted her knee.

"How are you doing, Button?" He asked.

Jenny swallowed hard before answering, "I'm fine."

"You are?" He gave her a skeptical look.

"Why do you ask?"

"Well, this is the thing, everyone is worried about you. Love told me she thinks something is the matter. Jimmy and Paul said so, too. Jimmy told me he was gonna come out here this morning and talk to you. I told everyone to just hold on, it's a Dad's job to check in on his little girl when something's the matter." Here he paused and gave her another quizzical look. "So tell me, Button, what's the matter?"

Big, fat tears welled up in her eyes and her throat tightened as she tried to keep from crying. Her Dad put his arm around her shoulder and pulled her to him.

"Oh, Dad," Jenny said and burst into tears. He held her gently as she let out her grief and frustration. Soon her tears had turned to sniffles and he pulled a freshly ironed handkerchief out of his jacket pocket and gave it to her.

"Now, now," he said softly, "what's all this about?"

"It's everything," Jenny shrugged and let her hands flop into her lap.

"Everything?" He raised his eyebrows in mock surprise. "Now that is something to get upset over. Everything is a lot."

She smiled despite herself and shook her head 'no'. "Not everything."

"Let me take a few guesses and you tell me if I'm right," he said. She blew her nose into his handkerchief and nodded in agreement. "Does it have anything to do with that long haired fella?"

Jenny laughed a little then nodded, "A little."

"Okay, that's a piece of it." He squinted across the clearing, pondering what he was going to say next. "Does it have anything to do with Love?"

"Your Love?" Jenny sniffed as she clarified.

He nodded 'yes'.

"A little," Jenny said shyly. She didn't want to hurt her Dad's feelings.

"Okay, that's something I expected you to have trouble with," he admitted. Jenny was surprised that he wasn't surprised. He looked at her keenly, waiting. When she didn't say anything else he asked, "And what else, Button? What else is bothering you?"

Jenny's face crumpled as her grief took over. She lifted the handkerchief to her mouth trying to control her break down and succeeded only long enough to say, "And I miss Mom." Then she broke down, bawling like a baby into her Dad's shoulder. They stayed like that for a while, long enough for her sobs to mellow into sniffles. When she finally lifted her head to wipe her eyes and nose, her Dad had tears in his eyes too. He wiped them away with the back of his hand.

"I do too." He looked down at his hands then up at the sunshine filtering through the trees across the clearing. "You know, I think about your Mom every day, all day long really."

Jenny sniffed. She hadn't known that.

"It's one of the things that connected Love and I, we can talk to each other about our spouses. She lost her Carl and I lost my Suzanne and there's something nice about being able to talk about them when you think of them."

Jenny let that sink in before answering.

"I can see that," she said.

"I think I would have liked Carl if I'd known him," he acknowledged with a grin. "I'm sure Love and your Mom would have liked each other."

Jenny smiled at the thought of Love and her Mom picking out china for Thanksgiving dinner together and had to admit it seemed plausible. She sniffed again before conceding.

"She is nice."

"Yes, she sure is," he agreed. He smacked her knee warmly. "You know who else is nice?

"Who?"

"That long haired kid, what's his name?" He winked at Jenny and she felt fourteen again.

"Da-ad!"

"I'm gonna tell you something, Jenny, something I think you should know."

"Okay," she waited.

"Losing someone you love doesn't mean you have to feel sad forever. It's not a life sentence of mourning." He watched her as he spoke, making sure she was listening. "Your Mom wanted you to be over the moon happy when she was alive and she wants the same thing for you now that she has passed. It's fine to have memories and to cry when you need to." He squeezed her shoulder so she was squished into him. "And it's also fine to laugh and have fun, to make plans and even, if the right guy comes along, to fall in love."

A deep sense of comfort flooded through her body. She suddenly realized her shoulders had been tight and heavy, but now felt relaxed and light, as if she was ready to dance. Relief took over and what must have been pent up guilt simply slipped away.

They walked together back to the house. Jenny found herself looking for Aaron. She didn't see him anywhere outside or in the house when they went in to make breakfast.

Love was there, creating some kind of quiche she had found in one of the old cookbooks. She gave them one of her wide smiles when they came in the French doors.

"Was the sunrise beautiful?" She asked.

A happy glow took over Jenny's face and she gave Love a genuine smile, "It really was."

"There's coffee if you want some," Love offered.

She truly is a nice lady, Jenny thought as she poured a cup of coffee. Then, because she couldn't ignore his absence, she wondered where Aaron was.

## ❧ 14 ❧

Aaron didn't appear during breakfast and even though the table was full with Jimmy and his family, and Love and her Dad, it seemed to Jenny like there was a gaping hole in the room.

As they were clearing the dishes from the table Jenny posed the nonchalant, she thought, question, "Has Aaron already eaten?"

Love responded with an apologetic look then replied quickly, "He left really early, said he wanted to get a look at the big lakes north of here."

Jenny's stomach tightened with such force it made her feel sick. For a second she was afraid she might lose her breakfast. Love watched her with an empathetic smile. Jenny simply nodded and put the dirty dishes she was holding down on the counter. They landed with a clatter.

"Sorry," Jenny said, trying to hide her shaking hands by wrapping her arms around her stomach.

Love placed her hand lightly on Jenny's back and said quietly, "He'll be back later today." Jenny tried to act like his return meant nothing to her, but she wasn't fooling anybody.

"Aunt Jenny," Penny asked from the table, "Do you want to color with me?"

"Sure," she smiled at her niece as the little girl hurried out of the room to get her coloring supplies. She was thankful for the distraction.

It turned out Jenny needed to fill her entire day with distractions. Aaron didn't return until just before dinner was on the table, but he came bearing gifts. Everyone was full of smiles as he passed them each something out of a large paper tote bag. First up was Penny.

"Now, this is for you to share with your Dads," Aaron told her, his hand still hidden inside the bag where she couldn't see.

"Okay!" She agreed, her cheeks pink with excitement.

Aaron pulled out three sheep hand puppets. Two had ram horns, one with white wool and one with black. Then there was an adorable baby lamb puppet with soft grey wool and big doe eyes.

"Aww," Paul said, "It's our family!" He and Jimmy grinned at each other as Penny delighted putting the puppets on each of them and then herself.

"Thank you!" Penny told Aaron, always the sweet one.

"You're welcome," Aaron's face glowed, happy in his role as the giver of presents, like Santa come early. He was, by far, the handsomest Santa Jenny had ever seen. He dug in the bag again.

"Rudy," Aaron said, handing her Dad a beautiful wood handled chef's knife. "For your kitchen. And Love," he pulled a heavy cookbook out of the bag handing it to her. When she read the front she laughed out loud and turned it around for everyone else to see, 'Love is at the Table' was the title. "I couldn't pass that up!" He said as she gave him a hug and kiss on the cheek.

"Thank you, sweetie," Love said.

"You're welcome," he told her, then to both of them, "I really appreciate you inviting me here for the holiday."

"You're welcome anytime," Rudy told him.

There was a beat, a minuscule glitch in the casual fun vibe of the room. Then Aaron turned to Jenny. A hush fell over the room, or maybe it was her imagination, either way she couldn't tear her eyes away from him. His eyes shone as he stepped closer to her. They held her fast in their grip, so much so that she didn't look away to see what he held in his hands until he pressed it into hers. She blinked and looked down at a deep blue leather bound book. No, not a book, a journal, with script on the front that read 'Fill your paper with the breathings of your heart'.

"Oh," she said, a sweet sadness rushing through her.

Aaron tipped his head towards her, pieces of his blonde wavy hair tumbling down around their faces when he did. "It seemed to me you might fill up your other one pretty soon."

She beamed at him, the intimacy of his gift and the expression on his face made her a little faint. No words came to her, but she managed a quiet, "Thank you."

He leaned closer to her and she thought for a split second that he might kiss her cheek, like Love had kissed his. He didn't.

"You're welcome," he said quietly, and that was all.

The evening carried on and Jenny did not recover her voice. The urge to talk to Aaron came often. All night she wanted to pull him aside and sit with him in a quiet place to tell him that she thought she'd made a mistake, that maybe they could have a romantic relationship maybe even fall in love, that she really, really wanted him to kiss her. Even though the desire was there she couldn't find the right time or the right words. Every moment seemed frozen, untouchable, yet they went by so fast it was time to go to bed before she knew what had happened.

Her Dad and Love excused themselves first, worn out after a week of company. Paul and Jimmy said their hushed goodnights as Jimmy carried a sleeping Penny up the stairs towards their room. That left Jenny alone with Aaron in the front sitting room, watching the fire die down to embers. They were silent for a while. He was sprawled comfortably on the couch while she sat curled up in her mother's favorite chair. She didn't know what to say to him, but couldn't bring herself to leave. Finally she had a thought.

"Thank you again for the journal. I really love it."

He shifted his gaze from the fireplace to her, taking a moment before answering, "I'm glad." His smile was soft and tired. It occurred to her that he must be exhausted after driving up north and back today. She was keeping him up and probably making him uncomfortable. This was his makeshift bedroom after all. He couldn't go to sleep with her sitting there watching him. Embarrassment flooded over her.

"I should get to bed," she said, unfolding herself from the chair.

He sat up, too, then stood when she stood. For some reason this action infuriated her. They weren't at a formal dinner, why was he acting like such a gentleman?

"Sure, it's late," was all he said.

"Yeah," Jenny snapped, "it is." She walked to the stairs and started to climb.

"Jenny," he said. Her stomach flipped at the sound of his voice speaking her name. So ridiculous, but she stopped anyway.

"Yes?"

"I'm glad we're going to be friends."

Hot disappointment shot through her heart, but all she could manage was a polite, "Me too."

## ❧ 15 ❧

The next morning was a bustle of activity as the whole house woke up and got ready for their long drives home. Breakfast was minimal, coffee was in abundance. This was a good thing, because Jenny hadn't slept a wink. Every moment she and Aaron had spent together over this past week kept running like a movie through her mind, keeping her awake through the night. Nevertheless, it was time to leave this vacation behind and move on with life. She was glad she'd had some time to get to know Love and be with her Dad and brother and his family...and she was glad to have met Aaron even if they weren't meant to be together.

That's what people did, right? Be glad about the experience no matter if it ended with their heart crushed into a million pieces.

Jenny packed, adding her stack of journals on top of her folded clothes. She placed her Mom's peacock card carefully sandwiched carefully between her green journal and the blue one Aaron had bought her as a sign of their friendship. She sighed, resigned to leaving. There was nothing more to do here. She'd already ruined her best chance at love, may as well go home.

Downstairs Penny was running wild as Jimmy and Paul hauled luggage to their car. Jimmy would be riding home with them instead of with Jenny as he and Paul and their daughter were now a reunited family. She would be driving home alone, of course.

Aaron was still in his pajamas deflating the air mattress. No doubt he would wait until they all left so he could pack and leave in peace. Though she was irritable at not having any sleep, she still found herself watching him, appreciating the way he looked, the way he moved. He wore a pair of flannel Pj's that hung dangerously low on his hips and a very faded orange Broncos T-shirt. Yet, somehow, with his hair tumbled on top of his head in a mop, he still managed to look good. She didn't know if she could forgive him for that.

They found themselves alone for a moment in the kitchen while she was filling her thermal mug with coffee to go. He sat on the opposite side of the kitchen island watching her, his eyes rimmed red as if he, too, had not gotten a good night's sleep. Jenny clicked the lid on her cup and looked around the kitchen. It was time for her to go.

"Well, I guess this is it," she said.

He nodded and yawned his response, "I hope you have a good trip home."

Then he stood up and jogged around the island to where she was, opening his arms to her for a goodbye hug. After a tiny hesitation she let him wrap her up in a comfy pajama embrace. Her cheek pressed against the muscles in his chest and his strong arms were warm and safe as he held her for a long moment.

As the pulse of his heartbeat fluttered against her cheek and the ends of his beard tickled her forehead her mood softened. Suddenly sleepy, she wished she could crawl back into her bed upstairs, taking the hug with her. Instead, she said the first thing that came into her mind.

"I'm sorry I said no."

Her voice was muffled against his T-shirt.

He pulled away from her. "What did you say?"

Jenny looked up into his face. Even bloodshot his eyes were beautiful.

"I said I'm sorry I said no. I think I would have liked to kiss you," she answered.

Aaron stared at her for a moment, not saying anything. Then he opened his mouth as if to speak only to shut it again.

Jenny pulled away and grabbed her coffee cup. It was obvious this was not a conversation he wanted to have and now she just wanted to get away.

"Goodbye, Aaron," she said, and walked out of the kitchen.

Once outside, her Dad helped her get her suitcase into her trunk and she busied herself with saying goodbye to Penny. She had to promise her niece that she would come to see them for Christmas and her birthday, which was right after Christmas. Jenny promised. Then she hugged Paul and Jimmy goodbye, happy they were getting back together, feeling melancholy taking over at the same time.

She looked for Aaron, but he was nowhere to be seen. He must be packing and thanking his lucky stars he avoided any kind of connection to her, a crazy person who doesn't know what she wants. He was probably thrilled he'd dodged that bullet. She felt tears pressing at the back of her throat and eyes, but swallowed hard and held them back long enough to say goodbye to her Dad and to Love.

She hugged them both and managed to smile and wave at them as she pulled away from the house. Paul and Jimmy had already gone. Aaron was still hiding from her. She was all alone.

The tears came once she started down the winding road. Flowing hot and heavy down her cheeks, they were the tears of a broken heart. The scenery was grim. Most of the trees in the surrounding woods had lost their leaves, leaving mostly gnarled branches spreading for as far as she could see. They looked like she felt...empty. She didn't know how she was going to get through the next few hours driving and crying at the same time. She didn't know how she was going to get through the rest of her life knowing that she'd pushed Aaron away.

Ahead she saw the covered bridge, one of the places Aaron had wanted to kiss her, one of the moments that was forever lost to her. She was crying so hard now she had to slow the car down as she entered. Moving slowly through the bridge, she wiped the tears from her eyes with the back of one hand in an attempt to keep from crashing her car into the ancient wooden walls.

Suddenly she saw a flash of orange move in front of her car and a loud thump sounded on the hood. She screamed and slammed on her brakes. In an instant her fear turned to surprise when she saw Aaron standing in the middle of the road in front of her leaning against her hood as if he had stopped her car by force. She stared at him, shocked. He said something that she couldn't hear. She put the car in park and stepped out.

"I have a question for you," Aaron said, he was breathing hard. He must have run all the way from the house to catch her here.

"What are you doing? I could have killed you!"

Aaron shrugged, unconcerned. Jenny looked him up and down. He was still in his Pj's, but had added a pair of boots pulled hastily on, his flannel pajama bottoms crumpled at the top of them. Jenny was speechless. Aaron was a little out of breath, but he had something to say.

"I have a question for you," he said again.

She half-laughed, half-snorted. This was ridiculous. Her car was idling in the middle of the covered bridge with its nose sticking out one end and this wild haired barely dressed Viking looking man blocking her path demanding to ask her a question.

He raised his eyebrows at her, waiting for a response.

"What?" She asked, because she basically had no other choice.

He lifted his hands off of her car and straightened to his full height. Locking his eyes on hers, he took the few steps between them and was almost instantly standing directly in front of her, so close she could feel the warmth of his skin emanating through his T-shirt.

He reached up and touched her cheek, pushing her hair back behind her ear, exactly like she had wanted to do to him for so long.

"Jenny," he said softly. He let his gaze wander from her eyes to her lips and drop to her chest that was lifting up and down rapidly with shallow, excited breaths. He smiled and raised his icy blue eyes to look into hers again. "Jenny," it was almost a whisper.

She tried to answer, but her voice caught in her throat. He let his hand move from her hair, running his fingers along the side of her neck, over her shoulder and down her arm until he had her hand in his. Electric shocks shimmered through her body at his touch. She waited.

"I have a question," he said again, his voice cracked as he said it. His own feelings overtaking him.

"What?" She asked, her own voice matching his in a whisper.

"Can I kiss you?"

She sucked in her breath as a shiver went down her back.

Placing her hand on his chest to steady herself, she answered, "Yes."

The corners of his eyes crinkled into a smile. His hands moved to her waist, wrapping around her, steady and firm. Then, finally, he dipped his head down and his lips were on hers. Softly, so softly, he kissed her, holding her tightly to him as he did.

His beard and mustache tickled her cheeks and chin. She moved her hands up his chest and around his neck, pushing her fingers into his thick, wavy hair. Still, he kissed her, drinking her in. Sunshine filled all of the dark places in her heart. Her sadness and loneliness dissolved and trembled deep inside her core before drifting outward through her skin and the tips of her fingers, floating away. What remained was pure joy and passion.

He pulled his mouth away from hers and looked down into her face, his eyes shining, "That's one."

"One?"

"I told you, I want to kiss you a thousand times."

Her brow wrinkled into a frown. "A thousand?"

He nodded, a questioning look on his face.

She traced her finger along his temple and cheek, smoothing over his mustache and finally letting it rest on his lips, those fantastic, insistent lips. Then she grinned, her eyes mischievous, and said, "At least!"

Aaron threw his head back and laughed. Then he kissed her on her mouth, on her nose, on her cheeks, finally burying his face into her neck. He lifted her up, twirling her around in a joyful hug. She laughed and held tight to him. Her Viking, her wild haired man with the piercing blue eyes, her gift from Love.

THANK you for reading Love is at the Table! If you enjoyed this book you may enjoy the other books in the series...

Enchanting Eve - Halloween Romance
Mistletoe Madness - Christmas Romance
New Year in Paradise - New Year's Eve Romance

YOU MIGHT ENJOY Darci's Dream Come True series. The first book, Her Scottish Keep is a fun and flirty romance set in the Scottish Highlands...a clean and wholesome contemporary Scottish love story :)

# EPILOGUE

Jenny stood in front of the mirror in her bedroom at the Lake House, taking a minute to herself before one of the biggest events of her life began.

Her dress was pure white. A beautiful, lace bodice fit smoothly over her curves and an off the shoulder cut made her shoulders look especially graceful. The lace turned to French tulle at the waist, which fell softly and elegantly to the floor. She did not wear a veil. She had decided that would be too much for the small ceremony they had planned, but her hair was swept up into a loose bun held in place with crystal encrusted hair combs and hair pins decorated with tiny crystal rosebuds.

Jenny touched the simple pearl necklace at her throat and smiled. Her mother had worn this necklace when she married her Dad, and he had proudly gifted it to her when she and Aaron arrived at the Lake House last week for Thanksgiving and to begin their final wedding preparations. Then Aaron had surprised her with matching drop pearl earrings he bought for her to match. So sweet, the two of them working in cahoots together to make her wedding day that much more meaningful. She was so lucky to be so loved.

She checked off the list quickly in her mind. Something old, her necklace, something new, her earrings, something borrowed, her crystal rosebud hair pins were actually Love's, which she'd offered happily for the occasion. And something blue, she lifted her skirt slightly to reveal a slim, aquamarine anklet that Jimmy and Paul had found on one of their weekend getaways. She was covered from head to toe with love, of that she was certain.

There was a soft knock on the door announcing Jimmy and Paul's arrival.

"Come in," she said, turning towards the door. Her brother and his husband stepped into her room, looking sharp in their matching red and black checked waistcoats with white rose boutonnieres.

"We have your flowers," Jimmy said as he carried a tasteful bouquet of orange lilies mixed artfully with red and white roses to her. "Jen," he looked her up and down, smiling the whole time, "You look beautiful!"

"You're gorgeous, darling!" Paul added, giving her a kiss on the cheek. "This is going to be a wedding of epic beauty."

Jimmy nodded as he handed her the bouquet, "You should see that boy of yours." He gave one of his low whistles and Jenny giggled.

"He looks grand, darling, like a Viking who won the lottery!"

"Or a fur trader who has become a prince!" Jimmy added.

"Aunt Jenny," Penny called as she came through the door. Six-years old now, Penny wore an adorable deep orange flower girl dress and carried her own mini version of Jenny's bouquet. "Grandpa says we're ready!" Her eyes shone with excitement, reflecting Jenny's feelings perfectly.

A cello played as Aaron's father escorted his mother down

the stairs into the sitting room that had been emptied of furniture, filled with folding chairs and decked out in white lights, candles and so many flower garlands the smell of roses hung sweetly in the air. They were followed by Paul escorting Penny down the stairs, then Jimmy escorting Love, who looked radiant in a deep rose colored dress.

Finally, Jenny's Dad took her arm at the top of the stairs. He kissed her on the cheek and patted her arm saying, "You are a vision, Button. You're Mom is so proud of you right now, I can feel it."

"I love you, Dad," she said, as she kissed him on his cheek. She blinked back tears.

"Ready?" He asked. She nodded and he walked proudly with her down the stairs to the small group of friends and family that were already seated, and to the man she was going to marry who stood waiting for her.

Aaron's eyes were always brilliant, always bright when he looked at her, and always full of love. But Jenny had never seen them quite as shining and intense as they were on this day, their wedding day. He stood tall and masculine in narrow black slacks, crisp white shirt and his own waistcoat of pure black. His boutonnière had red and orange roses, as he was the groom. And an impressive groom he was.

His wavy mane of blonde hair was loose except for the very top that was pulled back off of his face. He had trimmed his beard to the length she liked the best, and she thought he had never looked more handsome than he did in this moment.

Her walk down the aisle was not long, but it seemed like forever before she was finally standing next to him. Her father ceremoniously gave her hand to Aaron then sat down with Love. Aaron's warm, strong hand held hers and did not let go throughout their vows.

When he placed the shining wedding band on her finger,

slipping it up to nestle next to the princess cut diamond engagement ring he'd given her just a few months before, Jenny's heart swelled with love and joy.

When it was time for them to kiss as husband and wife, Aaron took her by the waist and turned her to him, drinking her up with his eyes before he leaned down and kissed her sweetly on the mouth. The small crowd clapped and cheered and Aaron leaned back, looking at her with a brilliant smile.

"That's one! Our first married kiss," he said. Jenny laughed, her happiness overflowing.

"We're going to lose count!" She exclaimed.

"I hope so," Aaron replied and took her in his arms again.

She was his, utterly and completely, and he was hers just the same.

THE END

If you're in the mood for a Christmas romance, get your copy of Charlotte's Christmas Charade the first book in A Sugar Plum Romance series – antics of chefs who get in over their heads at Christmas time and end up in charming holiday love stories!

# ALSO BY DARCI BALOGH

## Love & Marriage Contemporary Romance (Box Set - best bang for your buck!)

Steamy, emotional, relatable characters, these older woman, younger man romances are both racy and romantic.

1. The Quiet of Spring

2. For Love & For Money

3. Stars in the Sand

# ABOUT THE AUTHOR

Darci Balogh is a writer and indie filmmaker from Denver. She grew up in the beautiful mountains of Colorado and has lived in several areas of the state over her lifetime. She currently resides in Denver where she raised her two glorious, intelligent daughters to functioning adulthood. This is, by far, one of her highest achievements. She has a love-hate relationship with gardening, probably should dust more, adores dogs and is allergic to cats.

Darci has been a writer since she was a child and enjoys crafting stories into novels and screenplays. Big surprise, some of her favorite pastimes are reading and watching movies. Classic British TV is high on her 'Like' list, along with quietly depressing detective series and coffee with heavy cream.

Printed in the USA
CPSIA information can be obtained
at www.ICGtesting.com
LVHW090939151024
793791LV00002B/68

9 781943 990313